Sean Michael

THE LIBRARIAN'S GHOST

DREAMSPUN BEYOND

PUBLISHED BY

DREAMSPINNER
PRESS

Published by
DREAMSPINNER PRESS

5032 Capital Circle SW, Suite 2, PMB# 279,
Tallahassee, FL 32305-7886 USA
www.dreamspinnerpress.com

The Librarian's Ghost
© 2018 Sean Michael.
Editorial Development by Sue Brown-Moore.

Cover Art
© 2018 Alexandria Corza.
http://www.seeingstatic.com/
Cover content is for illustrative purposes only and any person depicted
on the cover is a model.

Paperback ISBN: 978-1-64108-104-7
Digital ISBN: 978-1-64080-738-9
Library of Congress Control Number: 2018934232
Trade Paperback published October 2018
v. 1.0

Printed in the United States of America
∞
This paper meets the requirements of
ANSI/NISO Z39.48-1992 (Permanence of Paper).

Often referred to as "Space Cowboy" and "Gangsta of Love" while still striving for the moniker of "Maurice," **SEAN MICHAEL** spends his days surfing, smutting, organizing his immense gourd collection and fantasizing about one day retiring on a small secluded island peopled entirely by horseshoe crabs. While collecting vast amounts of vintage gay pulp novels and mood rings, Sean whiles away the hours between dropping the f-bomb and pursuing the *Kama Sutra* by channeling the long-lost spirit of John Wayne and singing along with the soundtrack to *Chicago*.

A longtime writer of complicated haiku, currently Sean is attempting to learn the advanced arts of plate spinning and soap carving sex toys. Barring any of that? He'll stick with writing his stories, thanks, and rubbing pretty bodies together to see if they spark.

Website: www.seanmichaelwrites.com

Blog: seanmichaelwrites.blogspot.ca

Facebook: www.facebook.com/SeanMichaelWrites

Twitter: @seanmichael09

By Sean Michael

DREAMSPUN BEYOND
THE SUPERS
#6 – The Supers
#29 – The Librarian's Ghost

DREAMSPUN DESIRES
THE TEDDY BEAR CLUB
#39 – The Teddy Bear Club

Published by **DREAMSPINNER PRESS**
www.dreamspinnerpress.com

Chapter One

FOR all the Wexford House was two stories with a warren of a basement, there wasn't a lot of square footage. The Supernatural Explorers had examined the place thoroughly over the last three weekends, and Will Gregson felt like he knew each of the rooms inside and out. There was nothing new to find here.

It was definitely a creepy place. Old and abandoned with most of its original furniture after the owner's family—four daughters, three sons, two of their wives, four grandchildren, and his wife—were all wiped out by influenza. That the old man hadn't also died was a miracle. Or a curse, depending on which story you read. Rumor had it that his mistress had been a witch, and when he abandoned her, she protected him from the sickness that ravaged his family so that he would live the rest of his days alone and mourning. It was a nasty story, but one that persisted through the years.

The house was said to be haunted by Wexford's family, which was why they were here. Sure, they were hoping to concentrate on "gay ghosts," but there were only so many haunted places, so they were doing what they could when they could. Surely those types of cases would come, and when they'd made a proper reputation for themselves, they'd be called in from far and wide to check out gay hauntings. In the meantime, ghosts were ghosts, and they were happy to investigate, especially if the place was in the vicinity.

So far, the only thing they'd found at the Wexford House was disintegrating furniture and the bodies of various animals that had made their way into the place. Most of them had been dead for long enough that they didn't smell anymore. Hell, plenty weren't even identifiable. Though the one raccoon in the master bedroom had been fresh. Pretty damn gross. And while Will might have been morbidly fascinated with something like that as a boy, it wasn't something he enjoyed now that he was a grown man.

The dust was playing havoc with his sinuses too. They'd disturbed a lot of it during their explorations. That they weren't the first ones to do so had been apparent as well, and there were plenty of places where the dust was less thick in variously shaped spots—little circles and squares on the mantel and tables, spots where one might have expected to find various knickknacks. No doubt the place had been ransacked. Which sucked because when thieves stole pieces of history and the Supers—as they called themselves for short—couldn't find any ghosts, they could have maybe found some interesting museum pieces. It appeared the Wexford place had neither ghosts nor artifacts, so they were doing one last run-through to make sure they hadn't missed anything.

A low creaking noise sounded from upstairs, followed by tapping on glass. Will shivered. He knew it was the wind in the trees and the branches hitting the house—it was especially creepy when they tapped at the windows—but that didn't make it much better.

"Let's take one last sweep upstairs where that sound is coming from," Jason suggested.

"Yeah, the master bedroom was the only place where I got any sort of hit." Blaine led the way, moving slowly to try to mitigate how noisy the stairs were.

Personally, Will didn't think there were any ghosts to scare off with creaking stairs, but it didn't hurt to be as stealthy as possible. He avoided the big squeak on step three but managed to forget about the sixth stair until he was on it and it moaned beneath his weight. All four of his companions whipped around to stare at him, and he gave them an apologetic smile. He hadn't done it on purpose. Blaine was clearly biting the inside of his cheek while Flynn and Jason chuckled nearly soundlessly. He grinned back and put his finger in front of his lips. "Shh."

That set them all off, and they abandoned not making any noise in favor of their laughter and getting up the stairs quicker.

"Okay." Blaine turned to face him once they'd made the upstairs landing, and Will focused the camera on his friend's face. "We're in the Wexler House for the last time. We're hoping to communicate with what we think might be an entity in the master bedroom. Wexler's wife and most of the children supposedly died in the very bed that continues to dominate the room. We have our EMF readers at the ready, along with the infrared filter on the second camera. If there's anything to find, we're going to do exactly that. Find it. Document it. Deal with it if possible." Blaine turned back to peer into the master suite. "Will, why don't you and Darnell go in and do a scan of the room? Then Jason, Flynn, and I will follow."

Will nodded, keeping his voice off the audio, which would make it easier in postproduction. (Look at them, having postproduction now!) Despite the last few houses having been disappointing from a ghost perspective, the Supers were doing well. He focused on what the camera was seeing and stepped into the doorway. He did a long pan and scan from the door all the way around and back to it. He didn't see anything that looked like anything but shadows on the floor and back wall, but he was filming straightforward shots. Jason or Darnell could be picking something up on the more sensitive equipment.

Blaine and Flynn came in last and spread out across the room, Flynn going toward the window where the tapping was coming from while Blaine headed for the bed where the deaths had purportedly occurred. Blaine had his head tilted in what Will thought of as his listening stance. He waited, following Blaine with camera, holding his breath as if the sound of his breathing would disturb Blaine at work.

They all waited, hushed and still, as Blaine slowly moved around the bed. Even the tapping at the window had ceased, an eerie silence settling around them. The tension built, and Blaine froze, leaning in to look at something, though Will wasn't sure what. He certainly wasn't seeing anything.

All of a sudden came a terrible groaning, making them all jump.

Flynn laughed, the sound a touch strained. "That's the wind in that big willow." The branches began tapping at the window again, stronger than ever the breeze picked up outside.

Blaine sighed and nodded. "Yeah, it's nothing but the wind as far as I can tell."

"The instruments are pretty damn quiet too," Jason noted. "Do we need to go back to the basement one last time, or should we call it a night?"

"The ground is really uneven down there." Will had almost twisted his ankle on the dirt floor, and Blaine had actually fallen when he'd tripped over an unexpected rise between rooms.

"I don't feel anything at all, not even that small hint of something I felt the first time." Blaine shrugged. "Not proof of a lack of ghosts, of course, but this is our seventh day out here, and we've had nothing on any of the equipment either."

The sound of a stomach growling punctuated Blaine's words, and they all laughed.

"When the scariest thing in the room is Flynn's stomach, the best thing we can do is pack up and go get pizza." Jason made his pronouncement and headed back downstairs, the rest of them trooping along after him.

Will kept filming until they'd not only left the house but were back at the van. Once there, he did one last panoramic shot of the property before turning off the camera and packing it up.

PAYNE MacGregor watched his pot of soup, waiting for it to begin simmering. He didn't want it to boil over. Hell, he didn't want to turn his back on it in case the thing went flying across the room and sprayed everything with hot soup either. It was tomato too, which would be hell to clean up.

Truthfully, he was at his wit's end. At first he'd thought he was being absentminded, forgetful. Then he'd begun to wonder if he was losing his mind. None of the workers seemed to notice anything wrong. But he put that down to their being transient. They weren't there day after day like he was and were hardly likely to notice books and dishes being moved. Things flying across the room seemed to be reserved for him too. And that was harder to put down to his imagination. It wasn't like things were simply falling off shelves or tables; they were getting some distance.

Then he'd overheard arguments between some workers over items taken out of toolboxes and hidden. No one claimed ownership of these "practical jokes," making him think they weren't practical jokes at all but the work of the same... well, ghost—he was embarrassed to admit the assumption even to himself—plaguing him.

He took the soup off the stove the moment steam began rising from it and poured it into a bowl as his toast popped. Unfortunately, all but a corner of it was almost black. He was not one for toast *that* well done, so he put it in the garbage and took his bowl to the library to eat by the fireplace with his favorite books.

He had to wonder if he was simply being paranoid for believing that the burned toast was the responsibility of his ghost. On the other hand, the toast he'd had yesterday had turned out perfectly, and he was the only who could have changed the setting. Which he hadn't done.

One of the books went flying across the room, and he pretended he didn't see it, concentrating on his soup instead. He would do some work once he'd eaten, put in enough hours that when he did close his eyes, he'd fall asleep right away and wouldn't dream. At least he could hope that was how the evening played out, but it didn't mean that was what would happen. He pushed aside the niggling thought that he might have to do something about the strange things going on in the house at some point. Certainly if it got worse than the current annoyances. If not, well, he would deal with it.

As soon as he'd finished his soup, he set the bowl on his side table, right in the middle of it so it couldn't accidently fall to the floor. Then he grabbed his laptop and booted it up. In no time he was hunched over it, safely lost in his research.

Chapter Two

THE van pulled up in front of the converted barn where Blaine and Flynn lived, and they all spilled out, Darnell carrying the three large pizza boxes and Flynn holding the bags with their sodas.

"I'll be up in a minute," Will told them as he went around to the back. "I need to make sure we didn't leave anything behind." He was pretty sure they hadn't, but he wanted to rearrange how the equipment had been packed. When they finished up for the night, they tended to be wired and simply tossed everything into the back. That always made Will twitch. He might look like a rough-and-ready biker on the surface, but he liked everything in its place. It not only made it easier to find, but things were less likely to get broken or lost if they were properly stored.

While he might admit to himself that he probably had a touch of OCD, he wasn't going to say it out loud. He didn't want to be teased about it. His mother had considerably more than a touch of OCD, and until they'd gotten her meds sorted out, it had been debilitating.

It didn't take him long to manhandle the equipment out of the van, then put it back in so everything fit snugly in with everything else. In other words, he Tetrised it. Heavy stuff on the bottom, lighter stuff on top, holes where things could drop and get crushed kept to a minimum.

Satisfied, he locked up the van and headed inside. The place was nice and warm, and there was a cheery fire crackling away in the hearth. The guys were already a couple slices in on the pizza, but they'd started with the Greek pizza, which he didn't like thanks to the olives, so no harm, no foul.

He grabbed a beer and a couple slices of the meat lover's and sat on the dilapidated easy chair, careful not to rest his elbow on the right armrest as it was wonky. Blaine and Flynn were squished together on the loveseat like there wasn't enough room for both of them. It was adorable and nauseating at the same time. Jason and Darnell had set up residence on the couch—they knew Will liked the armchair. He wasn't tall, but he was a big guy, and the thing fit him perfectly with a little wiggle room on either side.

"I'm going to put the footage together for the Wexford House," Jason told them around a mouthful of food. "But I think we've pretty much concluded that there wasn't any ghost activity there. Just a lot of dust and noisy trees in the wind. Right?"

Will nodded his agreement along with the others. Wexford had been a bust, the third in a row after the incredible experience they'd had at the hospital. It wasn't surprising, really, but it was still a disappointment, and it wasn't helping their bid for a TV series any. He wasn't sure how many more episodes would get bought if all they were doing was debunking. Especially as they hadn't been able to find anything nearby that also fit into the gay ghosts' niche.

"So, I've got a job we might want to consider." Jason took a swig of his beer. "It's a little different from what we usually do, but it's a paying gig."

Flynn grinned. "I like getting paid. What's the deal?"

"You know the McGregor Mansion? Apparently the latest owner believes it's haunted, and he'd like us to come and investigate. He said something about an exorcism, so I do believe he wants us to get rid of the ghost."

"We're not priests."

Will recognized that expression on Flynn's face. That was pure stubbornness. Flynn was right too—they weren't priests. But they were talking about ghosts here and not demons, which didn't exist, right? He thought he knew where Flynn was coming from, though. Flynn's mom's ghost had hung around since he was little, keeping an eye on him. Not every ghost was bad, and they didn't all need to be gotten rid of.

Jason shrugged. "Like I said, it's a paying gig. And the owner is gay, by the way. Said so right up front. I guess that's part of why he chose us. He knows we want to film as we go, and there's a strong possibility we'll actually find a ghost, which we could really use. I think the production company would be willing to buy several episodes where we don't find anything if we can provide one every now and then where we do. Once we've confirmed a ghost, we can decide later whether we help him out or not."

Will had to admit he was all for getting paid. He didn't want to be a pizza-delivery guy for the rest of his life. "Let's do it. You did a fine job with the hospital, you know." The final cut of the show had rocked.

Darnell grabbed another slice of pizza and added before he shoved almost the entire thing in his mouth, "I'm in. Just point me in the right direction, and I'll shoot it."

"Good deal." Jason looked expectantly at Blaine and Flynn.

The two looked at each other like they had some psychic connection or something, which they didn't, right? Then Blaine nodded. "Okay, but if Flynn says the word, we're out."

Flynn took Blaine's hand, and their fingers twined together. It was sickening how in love they were. Okay, so it was less sickening and more that Will was fucking jealous. Who could blame him? He didn't have trouble getting laid or anything, but he wouldn't mind a steady lover, someone who made him as stupid as Blaine and Flynn were over each other.

"Okay," Jason said. "I'll call Payne MacGregor back and arrange for us to go in and check the place out. I won't promise more than that initially, but I'll have all the paperwork set up so we can get his John Hancock on the dotted line if we decide to go for it." He grabbed a beer and sucked half of it back.

Will took a Coke for himself, along with another piece of pizza. He had to drive the van home, so he was being good.

"Payne MacGregor sounds like a name from a children's book," Darnell said.

"Who would name their kid Payne?" was what Will wanted to know. "I bet he got the shit teased out of him growing up."

"God yes. Good old Payne MacG." Flynn started to giggle.

Jason rolled his eyes. "Get it all out of your systems now, boys. This guy is a client, okay? C-l-i-e-n-t. He's going to give us money to hunt the ghosts in his house, and it's one that's famously haunted at that. So if you're going to think 'Payne in the ass,' let's at least not call him that to his face."

Will snorted. They all fed off each other, as Jason very well knew. But they were professionals on the job. It was only when they were on downtime together that they let themselves go. Apropos of which Will couldn't resist teasing Jason. "No promises, but I'll try."

"Well, if anything comes out, say the ghost made you do it." Flynn was cracking up.

Will howled. "That's fucking perfect. I'm using that!"

Jason threw up his hands and started laughing too.

God, Will thought, these were the best friends on earth, the best guys a man could know. He grabbed his soda and held it up, waiting for everyone to notice and quiet down. "Here's to the Supernatural Explorers and a paying gig. I wouldn't want to do it with anyone else."

"No one else would take any of us," Jason said.

"Nope. Now raise your glasses and cheers with me, assholes."

Laughing, everyone clinked bottles with him. Yeah, the best group of crazy ghost hunters ever.

"Okay, okay." Jason tapped away at his laptop. "I did a little research before bringing this up to you guys, and I bookmarked the tabs with the best information. There's a lot of stories about the house—it is the oldest of its kind still standing, and the family that built it was filthy rich. It was constructed in the 1780s. They broke ground in 1782 in fact, and it took nearly five years to build. Apparently Angus MacGregor was a real harsh taskmaster, and the builders were treated worse than cattle. They lived in tents on the grounds while the building was being erected. They lost half the workforce to the cold the first winter, but despite the ground freezing and the snow, MacGregor insisted that the work continue through the winter months. He and his family lived in a hotel in town the entire time."

Will made a face. "He sounds like a real prince."

"You haven't heard the half of it yet."

"Go on, then, don't leave us in suspense." Darnell grabbed another slice of pizza, picking the toppings off and eating them bit by bit. Will tried not to watch.

"They lost fewer workers the second winter because by then the basement had been built and they were at least protected from the elements. From what I gather, food was the real problem at that point. MacGregor and his foreman rarely went out to the house with supplies during the winter months, and at least one worker had died of starvation by the time spring rolled around."

Wow. This was some real Scrooge-type stuff.

Jason continued. "So when the place was finally finished, Angus MacGregor moved his family in. He had a wife and eight kids, seven girls and a single boy. Eight legitimate kids that is. The servants lived in the basement—there's a half-dozen tiny bedrooms down there, along with the original kitchen."

"I'm surprised he gave the servants their own bedrooms." Will didn't think that sounded like this guy.

"It makes more sense when you learn that he slept with most of the female staff and had God knows how many illegitimate kids by them. There's no proof, but rumor had it that Mrs. MacGregor used to beat the girls he slept with, badly enough that not all of them carried their pregnancies to term."

"God, that's awful." Flynn looked horrified, as did Blaine and Darnell. Will felt the way they looked. Probably had that same stunned-and-not-in-a-good-way look on his face they did.

"The daughters were all married off, and the boy—Angus Junior—inherited when Senior died. Apparently there were mysterious circumstances surrounding his death. It's listed in the registry as natural causes, but many believe that the servants revolted. Maybe because two weeks before he died there was a fire in the basement that killed over half the staff. The fire never spread up to the main building—it stayed in the basement, and all the servants who were down there at the time died."

"Jesus Christ, no wonder the place is haunted." Will took a bite of his pizza because nothing was scary when you were eating pizza.

"There's certainly a long list of possible ghosts." Blaine took Flynn's hand again, and this time Will was definitely envious.

"You got anything else on the place?" Darnell asked.

"There's been a MacGregor there ever since. Direct descendants. What's really bizarre, though, is that there's always been only one son in each generation. And he's who inherited. I'm not sure if that was codified into the will or not, but that's how it's gone." Jason closed his laptop and set it on the coffee table. He stretched, long gangly legs spread out.

Blaine curled against Flynn's side. "I don't want to speculate too much before we get there. I don't want to contaminate anything. Better if I go in and feel it out first."

"That works." Jason grabbed his laptop again, opened it. "I'll email Mr. MacGregor and let him know we're available for next weekend, starting Friday evening."

"You guys want to stay for a movie or something?" Blaine asked. "We've got the good flavorings for popcorn again."

Darnell checked his watch. "Oh, I can totally stay."

"Me too." Will was game.

Jason nodded and grabbed some more Coke. Flynn got up to make popcorn while Blaine set up the movie, and they all settled in for the rest of the evening.

Chapter Three

PAYNE felt a little like an idiot, calling for a group of actors and con artists to come investigate the house, but he'd done his research—he was a trained librarian, after all—and there were a number of reasons to go with these guys. To start with, there was the fact that they advertised an interest in hauntings with a gay element, which he imagined meant that some or all of them were gay themselves. At any rate, even if they weren't, it had to mean they wouldn't object to having a gay client. Second, and most importantly, there were rumors that these boys had actually seen something. A real something.

God knew he had seen things.

He'd inherited the big old MacGregor manse two years ago, and he'd finally made it livable about three months ago. The fourth-floor attic was scary as hell. He wasn't sure what had gone on up there, and he wasn't sure he wanted to know, but it kind of looked like they'd padded the walls and maybe kept someone up there. The padded walls suggested that someone had been crazy. And as for the basement, where there were supposedly servant's quarters, he hadn't ventured down there yet. Every time he thought about checking it out, something seemed to come up to make him decide to put it off.

Payne had been handling the way things moved around and the opening doors and the way he kept hearing whispers, even the tossing of books and dishes. He put his head down and worked. But the whole pushing thing was new. Down the stairs, in the shower, across the newly mopped floor. That was too much.

The doorbell rang around ten minutes past their appointment meeting time of 7:00 p.m. He supposed he shouldn't be surprised that these so-called ghost hunters weren't punctual.

He opened the door, or tried to. The lock wouldn't turn. "Hold on! I'm coming!" He fought with it, but it was like the damn thing was rusted closed. Except he'd opened it not more than an hour ago, and it hadn't been rusty or sticky at all. "It's stuck!" Goddamn it. He hated this shit, and it was happening more and more.

"Your door is stuck?" The disembodied voice came from outside. "You want us to push or something?"

"The lock. Just a second." He stopped, closed his eyes, and took a deep breath; then the goddamned door unlocked. Just like that. Boom. Unlocked. Audibly. All on its fucking own.

He opened it, his hand trembling, and discovered a motley crew of five guys on his doorstep. The tall, lanky one with acne—he was what, fifteen?—thrust out his hand. "Supernatural Explorers, at your service."

"Payne MacGregor. Pleased to meet you." Breathe. In and out. The worst that could happen was that these guys were the con artists he was expecting, and they'd be on their way in short order.

"Pleased to meet you. I'm Jason. We spoke on the phone and via email. This is the team. Blaine, Flynn, Darnell, and Will. Can we come in?"

"Please do. Come on in." He held the door open wider, trying to find a smile. "Welcome to the MacGregor house."

"Thanks." A guy who looked more like a biker than a ghost hunter—what did a ghost hunter look like anyway?—was the first in. He'd always found the bad boy look hot, and this guy was no exception. He hadn't expected that. The guy offered his hand.

Payne reached out, and pure lightning seemed to jolt up his arm. "Oh. Static. Sorry."

The guy looked at his own hand, shook it a moment. "Weird. I'm Will, by the way. This is Jason, Darnell, Blaine, and Flynn. We're here for your ghost."

Strange, it was like Will had totally missed Jason introducing everyone not thirty seconds ago. Payne decided to ignore that—after all, what was a little more weirdness?

"Well, I hope you can find it." What was he supposed to do next?

"If there's really a ghost here, we'll find it." The guy named… Flynn, he thought… said cheerfully.

"I wouldn't have called if I didn't know there was a ghost." Whether these guys could tell or could do anything about, there was no doubt in his mind that the ghost existed.

"How about we sit, and you can tell us about it," Jason suggested.

"Of course. Please come into the drawing room."

"Dude, this place has a drawing room!" Someone—he wasn't sure who, though it was either Darnell or Blaine by process of elimination—was stupidly excited.

"This is wicked cool." Will was the first behind him, looking around, clearly fascinated. "We've always wondered about this house."

"I inherited it. I've been doing a ton of work." And research, making sure he got everything as accurate as possible.

Jason pulled a tablet out of his pocket. "Do you mind if I take notes?" When Payne shook his head, Jason bobbed his head. "Cool. So, the work—is it restoring-to-former-glory type of work or modernizing?"

"Restoration, barring things like electrical and plumbing, of course." That needed to come up to code. Besides, who wanted to live in a place without running water and proper heating?

"Well, then, I can't wait to see the place," Jason actually bounced in his seat on the couch. He was obviously really into the gothic style.

Payne nodded. "I'm happy to give you a tour afterward. Some of the rooms are less renovated, of course." At least they were all livable, though. Finally.

Will grinned at him. "We've been to all sorts of places, many of which have been condemned, so I think we'll manage less renovated."

"Well, I swear, there have been days I almost just had her torn down, but.... The fact is, the house has been in my family for generations, and I'm committed to saving it." He'd put more money into it than he could possibly recoup in a sale too.

"Oh, that would have been a shame," Flynn said. "She's got so much character. And your ghost might have reacted badly if you had."

"I didn't believe in ghosts until I moved here," he admitted. And if it hadn't been for the repeated, undeniable things going on now, he still wouldn't believe. But you could only reason away things flying across the room so many times before you had to admit there was more going on than shifting foundations.

"We do," Flynn said, and the others all nodded.

"If anyone is the skeptic among us, it's me." Will shrugged. "But I've seen enough that I'm not really a skeptic. I keep the guys honest, though."

"Good for you. I hope you prove me to be an idiot." He wasn't. He knew that.

The guy sitting next to Flynn, who looked like a real flower child, shook his head. "We won't. You've got a spirit. Maybe more than one."

Oh. Oh damn. "How—how do you know?"

"Blaine is our medium. He's more sensitive than any of us, and he can see spirits, communicate with them." Jason made a few notes. "What are you picking up, Blaine?"

"There's just…. Your grandmother lived here before you?"

"Well, yeah, of course. My grandfather left the house to me since my dad predeceased him, but my grandmother had a life interest, so I took possession after her death. That's all public record." He frowned, not at all impressed. These guys would have done their research, right?

"Easy." Will grumbled at him. "Give Blaine time. You don't need to start with the dismissive attitude right off the bat like that. You called us, remember?"

"Will," Jason hissed, glaring at the man.

"Right." Payne pulled himself up, stung. "Yes. This home has been in my family since it was built in the eighteenth century."

"I'm very sorry, Mr. MacGregor. We can be a bit protective of Blaine. The usual reaction to a medium is skepticism and disbelief. People assume he's conning them and act accordingly. But that reaction was uncalled for." The last was aimed at Will. Jason could glare.

Will sighed. "I'm sorry, I didn't mean to bite your head off. We are here to help. And obviously you believe or you wouldn't have called us. Right?"

Payne nodded, his lips tight. He did believe. He didn't want to, but he did. It would have been so much easier if he could dismiss everything that happened with logical explanations. But he couldn't.

"Then I hope you'll accept my apologies." Will sounded sincere enough.

"Sure." What did it matter? Seriously? He was going to be the librarian who believed in ghosts. The crazy guy who lived in the big old house.

"Okay, thank you." Will sat back, dwarfing the chair he had chosen.

"Why don't you tell us about your ghost, then," Jason suggested. "The things that you've seen and heard. Who you think it is, and why you think they're here."

"It started slowly, with things not being where I left them, different construction workers losing their tools." He'd thought it was a thief, honestly, at least until things started flying across the room and one guy had gotten hurt.

Jason made notes on his iPad. "Is there a reason why you didn't think it was some mischief maker—given that you've had people coming in and out, like the construction workers?"

"That's exactly what I thought at first, but then the accidents started happening." He wrapped his arms around his body, comforting himself. "That's when I started to worry."

"Accidents?" Jason asked, and all five of them leaned in.

"A cut hand. A window pane smashing into a worker. Then someone was pushed down the main staircase, and I saw it." The guy hadn't tripped—he'd clearly been pushed. Thank God he hadn't been badly injured, but the truth was he could have been killed.

"Did you see the person doing the pushing?" Jason asked.

"No. I mean, I don't think so." He'd seen the guy being pushed, but no pusher. Although he thought he'd seen something out of the corner of his eye, but maybe his brain had made it up, trying to make sense of it.

"So this isn't a happy haunting." Jason made more notes on his tablet.

"Do you have any idea why the entity is so mad?" Will asked. "I mean—you're bringing the place back to what it was. I would have thought that was a good thing."

"I don't have any idea. I brought in a priest, a psychic cleanser. I even did some things on my own." Lots of sage, salt on the window sills and across the doorways.

"A psychic cleanser?" Will nodded sagely. "No wonder you were questioning Blaine when he asked about your grandmother."

"I just…." He'd put everything into this house. Literally. If he left, he'd be penniless, but something was making it hard to stay.

"Go on. You just what? Anything you can tell us could be useful."

"This is my home. I can't leave. I'm going to outstubborn whatever it is."

Will chuckled. "You know what? I think I like you."

Darnell snorted. "I'm sure Mr. MacGregor will sleep at night now."

Will tossed one of the throw pillows at the guy. "Shut up."

Lord, they were young, but Payne thought the energy was good, friendly. Sort of wonderful.

"So what happens next?" Getting rid of his ghost problem tonight was probably not on the menu, though that would be nice. If these guys could get the ghost to leave, he'd be able to get a good night's sleep.

"We're going to explore the house," Jason said. "Check out all the rooms and see where we get the most activity. With your permission of course. Speaking of permission." Jason turned the tablet toward him. "We have a boilerplate agreement that basically says you won't hold it against us if anything happens to you or the house because of the ghost."

Payne frowned and started reading through the document. "Does this specify that you won't pull up floors or tear anything down?"

"*We* won't," Jason told him. "But we're not responsible if we piss off your ghost in our pursuits and it does the damage."

"Does that happen very often? Major destruction like that?" He had a contingency fund, but it wouldn't cover having to redo any of the renovations already completed.

Blaine responded this time, with a shrug. "No. A ghost has to be really strong to actually affect the physical world to that extent. But your ghost has already done a lot, so there's more likelihood that she's going to keep on doing stuff. I think the important thing is going to be to figure out why she's still here and why she's messing with you."

"She? How do you know it's a woman?" Payne thought so too, but he hadn't said. It made him feel a little stupid.

"It feels like a she." Blaine blushed softly but didn't back down. "I wasn't bullshitting you earlier when I asked about your grandmother. I feel a presence, a female presence. That's all I have so far, though."

"She wasn't evil. She was a little grumpy sometimes, but not mean." And some of the stuff that had happened—a lot of it—had been mean.

"She might just be trying to get in touch," Flynn suggested. "And while we're interpreting her actions as angry, she might not actually *be* angry. It could be she's unaware of exactly what she's doing, or that what she's doing is all she actually can do. For instance, maybe the push down the stairs was actually an attempt to make contact."

"You've been reading up." Blaine looked pleased.

Flynn smiled at Blaine, his expression warm. "Yeah, I have."

"Flynn's right," Jason said. "There's every chance she's simply trying to communicate and this is the best she can do. If we've got an agreement, we'll figure it out for you."

The other four nodded at Jason's words.

"Okay, but please be careful. I'm tapped out as far as reno budget goes."

Will narrowed his eyes. "You *can* pay us, yes?"

"You know what, I don't need this shit." He stood up, pissed off and a little hurt. These people were supposed to be here to help. "I haven't slept in days,

I'm living in hell, and last time I checked ghostbusters weren't renovations! Get out."

"Will!" Jason snapped, glaring at the man.

Will rolled his eyes and stood. "Take it easy, MacGregor—you said your budget was tapped out. I assumed that meant you were out of money, and you'll pardon me if things are tight enough for us that no cash in any budget means no cash period."

Jason stood too and put himself between Payne and Will. "We're very sorry we upset you. I really do think we can help you if you'll forgive our rough edges. If not, we'll totally just go."

"I'll pay for your gas and your time, but I have enough trouble at the moment without someone wandering around who obviously doesn't like me. How much do I owe you?" Payne felt like crying. Maybe he would take what he'd saved for this "investigation," go to a hotel for a few nights, and just sleep.

"You don't owe us anything, Mr. MacGregor. I'm sorry Will was such an ass. We don't dislike you at all, and we'd like to help you." Jason handed him a card. "Please call us when you need us more than you're upset with us."

Blaine stopped in front of him next. "Don't wait too long. There's a lot of energy here. More than I think your grandmother alone can account for, and it could get dangerous."

"Yeah, I know." He'd been living with it for months. "Please see yourself out."

Payne began to shake, and he took himself toward the kitchen. A cup of tea. That was what he needed. A nice, not-scary cup of tea. He went through the process of filling the kettle, putting it on the stove, and turning on the burner. Then he grabbed a cup before moving to the cupboard with the tea in it. He chose the chamomile, hoping it would help him sleep tonight. Going through the motions of making his tea was soothing in and of itself, and he'd stopped shuddering by the time he had everything set out.

The kettle was almost boiling when he heard footsteps. He tensed, waiting for whatever the ghost had ready for him next, then nearly jumped out of his skin when Jason spoke.

"I'm sorry, but we can't get out."

Chapter Four

WILL tried the front door again, but it wouldn't fucking budge. The handle would turn, but then nothing, not even a hint of movement. Well shit. He did it yet again, knowing that the eighth time was definitely not going to be the charm, but he couldn't stand there like an idiot and wait for the situation to change. So instead, he was standing there like an idiot, tugging at the door again and again. *Good one, Will.* He rolled his eyes at himself.

Blaine leaned against the hall wall, arms crossed over his chest, and watched. "We're not going anywhere. She wants us here."

"Yeah, well, her grandson doesn't." Will glared at the door. Handsome, arrogant MacGregor was a sexy son of a bitch. Wait. What? No. No, the guy was an ass. That was all.

"Why are you so mad at him, man?" Darnell asked. "He's been nothing but decent to us."

"You didn't catch the bit where he practically accused us of being frauds?" Will asked. He wasn't going to stand for anyone implying that Blaine was a rip-off artist and by extension that the rest of them were too. Every time he thought about MacGregor his blood started to boil. The guy was a class A a-hole.

"No...." Darnell actually blinked. "I didn't."

Will growled a little and tried the door again. Still not budging. Whoever the old broad was, she was making damn sure they stayed. And he knew it was a she because unlike certain douchebags, he believed in Blaine. "Well, he did. Making like Blaine didn't know what he knew from the entity, but from research. Like all we were doing here was trying to defraud him. It's not like he's paying us *that* much."

And maybe he'd been looking for it, looking for something after the shock he'd gotten when their hands had touched. Looking for a reason to grumble and growl. Still, there was something about the man that pissed him off. Payne MacGregor simply rubbed him the wrong way. He didn't need any reason more than that.

"Then he dismisses us like we're used tissues, and now his damn house won't let us out!" Will didn't understand why the others were so gung ho on this guy. Couldn't they see what was going on here?

"I did not!" MacGregor's voice seemed huge, and Will glanced over his shoulder to see that the man himself had arrived with Jason just in time to hear Will's last comment. "I wasn't mean!"

"Kind of what it felt like from this end," he countered.

Jason grabbed his hand and pulled—or rather yanked—him aside. "What the hell is wrong with you?"

"Nothing." He crossed his arms and glared.

"You're being an ass, man," Jason hissed. "This isn't like you at all. The guy is scared and exhausted, for fuck's sake. Look at him!"

He glared at MacGregor, but then studied him. Payne did look exhausted, the cheeks under the beard drawn and thin, eye bags dark and brutal. Maybe Payne hadn't been trying to be awful. And now Will felt like an asshole. He sighed and rubbed his face, then held out his hand. "Let's start over. Hi, I'm Will. We're here to help."

MacGregor blinked at him, obviously shocked. Had he really been that awful that the guy wouldn't even shake his hand now?

Will forced himself to keep his hand out, and bit back the angry comment on the tip of his tongue. Instead he said, "I'm just the cameraman and equipment manager, but Blaine here is the real deal." *Come on, take my hand before I decide to really take it personally and start snarling again.* This make-nice gesture wasn't his idea in the first place.

"Hey." MacGregor shook his hand, and the door popped open like magic.

Okay, that was more than a little spooky. "Christ, I might be just the cameraman, but even I can tell we're not alone here." Sure, ghosts were supposed to be spooky, but this seemed fucked up on a deeper level. Almost like Blaine-being-ridden-by-a-ghost deeper.

"I know." MacGregor looked so fucking lost.

Will realized he and MacGregor were still holding hands, and he let go. He didn't know what was wrong with him. He cleared his throat a few times, then looked at Blaine, at Jason. "We need any more info, or should we fire everything up and do a tour of the place?" Get moving. Do something other than just stand here by the door. That seemed like a particular waste of time, and if they weren't going to hunt this ghost, Will wanted out of the house.

"Mr. MacGregor? Should we stay?" Jason asked.

MacGregor looked at Will, and Will stared back, not saying anything. He'd apologized and admitted MacGregor needed their help. It was up to MacGregor to pull the trigger. If the dude didn't want them here, he'd be the first to throw up his hands, shout hallelujah, and head out the door.

MacGregor drew in a long breath. "Yeah. I'm making tea. Who wants a cup?"

"You have any pop?" Will asked. What he really wanted was a beer, but he could make do. His head was killing him, and he thought some liquid would help.

"I have a few cans in the fridge."

"Thanks, I appreciate it. I'm not a tea kind of guy." He wasn't even that into coffee, though he needed a cup or two first thing in the morning, like every other person out there.

Blaine grinned. "I am. And I've converted Flynn, so we'll take you up on your very kind offer. Let your ghost get used to us, though it seems she's determined to keep us here."

Payne led them into a gorgeous kitchen. Seriously—granite and stainless steel and tons of light. Will took in the appliances. Everything was brand-new, top of the line. There was room to move around, and the cupboards were all glass fronted so you could see the matching dishes stacked neatly row by row. The order of it appealed to Will, and he loved that it all matched. The cupboards at his apartment had wooden doors so you couldn't see the mismatched dinnerware inside, which worked for him.

"Nice."

"I think so. I love to cook, so…." Payne shrugged.

"I bet you do better than pizza every night." Not that Will didn't love pizza, because he did. The nights they had Blaine's mom's cooking were better, though. Hell, even Blaine and Flynn's cooking wasn't bad. Will didn't cook. He ate a lot of pizza and a lot of cereal.

"I have a pizza oven, but yeah, I don't do takeout much." Payne moved around the kitchen like he belonged there, like he knew what he was doing.

"Weird…." Will gave the boys a wink so they knew he wasn't being an asshole.

MacGregor's lips thinned, the muscles around them going tight. He even straightened his back some. "Well sure. I'm unique. That's not bad, right?"

Maybe he'd disliked MacGregor on sight, but this guy seemed to be just as happy to take him wrong too. Will tried not to let it make him growl again. "Not bad. I was just teasing." Maybe MacGregor didn't have a sense of humor.

MacGregor paused for a beat then took another breath. "Cool. How many teacups do we need?"

"Four of us, plus yourself," Jason told MacGregor. Traitor.

"And a soda. Feel free to grab one," MacGregor offered, pointing at the large stainless-steel fridge. He pulled five pottery cups out of one of the cupboards, along with a box of tea.

Will went over to the sweet fridge and opened it, spotting the pops easily. He grabbed a ginger ale. He probably didn't need anything with caffeine in it—he was already edgy. "Thanks." He managed to say it without sounding too gruff. Go him.

Everyone picked the tea they preferred from the box and MacGregor played mother, pouring water into each mug. It was so domestic. Quiet too. And weird. They'd only just met this guy, but they were standing around in the kitchen like it was something they did every evening. It felt almost… unnatural.

A glass fell out of the cupboard, bounced off the counter, and fell to the floor, where it shattered. Will jumped right along with the rest of them. Christ. That hadn't been a natural accident at all—he was sure of it.

"Oh stop it." Payne rolled his eyes and headed for a door that turned out to be the broom closet. He grabbed a broom and dustpan.

"Okay, so this has been going on for a long time if that didn't freak you out." Will was actually grudgingly impressed.

"There's a lot that freaks me out, but it's been throwing things for months." Payne swept the glass up and threw the shards away.

"Why did you wait so long to call us?" Jason asked. "Just kidding. We know you tried just about everyone else first."

Ha! He hadn't been the only one who'd noticed stuff like that. Will was about to say something, but Jason seemed to suddenly realize that he'd been rude all the way around.

Jason shook his head. "God, I'm sorry. We're not making a very good impression, are we?"

"Honestly, I didn't know people—groups?—like you really existed. Other than people who were faking it for television, I mean." MacGregor took a sip of his tea. "It didn't occur to me to check you out until I started finding reviews that indicated you guys had been dealing with real ghosts, or at least had come across stuff that could be linked back to actual events."

"Not all those TV guys are faking it. Exaggerating shit, yeah. But not all fake. We aren't." Jason grinned. "But it helps if you believe in the first place. And you definitely have an entity here."

Will had to chuckle. It was a ghost. They all knew that. Besides, he always thought calling it an entity made it sound like maybe they thought there was a demon or something infesting the house. And none of them believed in demons. Right? Right. They were ghost hunters. Not demon chasers. Demons did not need to be real, thank you very much.

"I know. I mean, I just need help with it. We have to live together, right? That's why I called the psychic. I thought we could communicate."

"You could have if the psychic had been real," Blaine noted. "She wants to communicate. That much is clear. And I don't think she wants you out."

"Well, I'm happy to…." MacGregor paused, clearly searching for the right words. "I don't know, reach an agreement."

"I guess the first step is figuring out what it is she wants—why she's here." Blaine sipped his tea, looking around the kitchen. He had that faraway look that usually meant he was seeing something that wasn't there for the rest of them.

MacGregor watched for a second, then took a few sips of his own tea, wrapping his hands around the cup like he was trying to warm them.

The rest of them observed Blaine, simply waiting for him to come back to them. They were used to this and would only interrupt him if he seemed to be in distress or forgot to breathe. That had happened once, and it had been the scariest fucking thing. Now they were careful not to let it happen again.

Blaine frowned, then shook his head. "She's not ready to trust us, I don't think."

"Well, why don't we have our tea and then let Mr. MacGregor show us around the place," Jason suggested. "I imagine we're going to get pretty familiar with it over the next few days at least."

"Are you going to want me to leave? I see on the television that's the way it normally works."

The kitchen door slammed closed, and they all looked at it.

"Nope," Blaine murmured. "I don't think this is going to work without you here."

"Huh. Okay." MacGregor sighed and sipped some more of his tea.

"Don't worry, we don't usually stay anywhere 24/7, and we'll only do that here if it looks like it's necessary." Jason pulled out the contract again. "I hate to be a nag, but if we're going to do this, we really need you to sign this."

"Right." MacGregor took the tablet, signed it, then handed it back.

"Thanks. We just need to dot all our i's and cross all our t's, you know?" Jason hit the button to turn the tablet off, and Will knew he was pleased to have all the paperwork completed.

"Sure. That makes sense." MacGregor leaned against the counter with his shoulders hunched and his head bent over his cup.

Will couldn't believe how defeated, how tired, MacGregor seemed.

"You've signed us up for the job now, MacGregor. We'll get things figured out, and you'll see—you'll be back to normal in no time." Will had faith in their little team.

"Never fear, the Supers are here," Jason added, chuckling.

MacGregor smiled at them, but the look was worried, tentative rather than relieved. "Right on."

"So how long have you been living here?" Flynn asked as they stood around the kitchen with their tea and pop.

"Just a few months. I had to do a lot to make it livable."

"How long have you been working to make it livable?" Flynn pressed.

Payne smiled. "A little over two years."

"A labor of love, then. So when did the weird stuff start?"

"Like I said, it was pretty early. I mean, there's no way to know for sure, especially as I wasn't living here yet. And at first I thought it was just coincidence or bad workers or… I don't know. Bad luck?"

"Yeah, I can see that. Did you believe in ghosts before any of this started happening?" Blaine asked.

"I hadn't really thought too much about it, if I'm honest. My experience with ghosts was directing people to Stephen King and Dan Simmons."

"And when did you decide what was happening wasn't bad luck but maybe something supernatural?" Blaine finished his tea and put the cup down on the table.

MacGregor sighed. "The worker being pushed down the stairs was the first time. Then I started sleeping here. It seems like everything went crazy then."

"Did you feel threatened? Do you have any inkling why the presence is here?"

Will studied MacGregor as Jason went through all his questions, wondering if anyone else felt the way the room was growing slowly colder. He didn't know what it meant, but it definitely wasn't natural, and it seemed to link to whatever was going on here.

"I just felt... like someone was always watching, like there was always pressure." MacGregor shrugged. "Sometimes it felt almost nice. Other times it was... not comfortable."

"Pressure? Was it directing you in a certain direction? Like, did you feel you had to do something— general or specific?" Blaine seemed to have an endless supply of questions, but Will knew he was just gathering as much information as he could. They usually didn't have someone who'd been living with the ghost when they explored a haunted place.

MacGregor shrugged, obviously uncomfortable. "Just.... Just pressure, you know?"

"You sure you can't describe it better than that?" Blaine asked. "We're just trying to narrow things down, see what we can make work."

"It's like someone's on me, leaning on my shoulders, all the time," MacGregor admitted. "Only now and then it stops. It's usually not as bad in my bedroom, but otherwise, it's always there."

"That sounds uncomfortable." Will wouldn't like that. Hell, he didn't like being in this house at all, and he'd only been putting up with it for a short while.

Blaine agreed. "It does."

"It is. It's exhausting." MacGregor put his cup down, the thing rattling for a second. "So you guys want the tour?"

"Yeah, I think it's time for it. Sooner we get a feel for the place and your ghost, the sooner we can help you." Blaine took his cup to the sink and set it down.

Will grabbed his camera. "I'm going to film this, okay?" He knew they had permission, but he was trying to be nice. See? He didn't have a hate-on for this guy. He didn't know what Jason was riding him about.

"That's the point for you guys, right?"

"Even if we never use the footage for a show," Flynn explained, "it helps us if we can go back and sync up what the rest of the equipment and our senses tell us with what shows on camera." He took out the EMF reader. "This detects spirits."

"Really? How?"

"It picks up electromagnetic frequencies," Jason explained, so patient. "It'll pick up live wires and such too, so we have to pay attention."

"Huh." MacGregor examined the EMF reader.

"Come on, MacGregor." Will shouldered the camera. "Give us the grand tour."

"Well, this is the kitchen. The pantry and laundry are through here, as is the back entrance." MacGregor opened the door to reveal the two rooms, which were loosely connected by an archway and dimly lit by moonlight streaming in the window in the back door.

They left the kitchen and only went a few steps into the hall before MacGregor stopped at another door. "This goes to the basement." The door was locked with a heavy padlock.

"Is there something dangerous down there?" Jason asked as Blaine put his hand on the door.

"There's no reason to go down there." The words were almost toneless.

Frowning, Will focused the camera in on MacGregor. He looked... glassy-eyed, for a start.

"Why not?" Jason asked.

"Come to the parlor and the library." MacGregor walked away from the basement door, and his face cleared.

Will turned the camera on the guys. "I wasn't the only one who saw that, right?"

Jason shook his head. "That was weird. Like, Blaine weird."

"Hey!" Blaine said it, but it was Flynn who bopped Jason on the arm.

Jason grinned at Will. "Stay with him, man. Let's get everything."

Will went after MacGregor, catching up with him halfway down the hall. The guy really wanted to avoid the basement. "Where to next?"

"This is the parlor." He waved through a doorway at a smallish room cluttered with a mishmash of items. I'm not sure yet what I'm going to do with it. That's why the extra furniture is here, so it's a little crowded. But the library is fabulous."

"You have a library?" Will asked. "Like, an honest-to-God library?" People had those in their houses?

"I'm a librarian. I do have an honest-to-God library."

"Yeah, but in your *house*. Lead the way." Will was impressed in spite of himself.

The library, which could be reached either through the parlor or through another door down the hall, *was* amazing, filled with shelves of books, a huge desk, and vast leather chairs. Will whistled. This was an old-fashioned, old-manor library. Now he regretted his "are you sure you can pay us" comment. MacGregor was clearly loaded.

"This is the room I've wanted to restore as long as I can remember. I've put so much into it." MacGregor ran his fingers along the top of one of the chairs, then went to the shelves against the far right wall and touched them lovingly. This guy liked his books. A lot.

"So you've been here before you inherited it. Which makes sense as it's a family home. When was the first time you came here?" Blaine asked.

"Oh, I must have been a baby. This is my paternal grandmother's house. My parents divorced when I was five, and I came much less often after that."

"Do you ever remember feeling a presence here? Either before or after she died? Did you have an imaginary friend who seemed particularly real?" Blaine focused in on MacGregor as he asked the questions.

"Bonzi. I called her Mama Bonzi." MacGregor looked amazed. "How did you know?"

"Because maybe she wasn't so imaginary. Kids have a stronger connection to the supernatural because they haven't been taught not to believe yet. Tell us about Mama Bonzi."

"She was a little gnome with a wooden spoon who lived under the bed. She made me laugh."

"A gnome with a wooden spoon? That's adorable." Will chuckled.

"So she was friendly," Blaine noted. "Did she ever go home with you, or was she just here?"

"I don't remember. She was gone by the time I went to school—but my parents divorced, we moved, I grew up. You know?"

"I do know. That's how it goes for most people. You grow out of ghosts." Blaine shrugged. "Some of us don't. It's helpful, though, to know that she's localized here. And that there was an entity here before your grandmother died."

"They found her at the bottom of the stairs. She'd been dead for a week," MacGregor delivered the news baldly. Just laid it out there.

"Jesus fuck." Will shook his head. He hated hearing that kind of thing. Bad enough to die alone, but to be left there that long was worse.

"At the bottom of the basement stairs?" Jason asked, jerking his head back in the general direction of the padlocked door.

MacGregor shivered but didn't answer. "The bedrooms are upstairs."

"Did he just duck the question?" Will whispered.

"He did," Jason cleared his throat. "Mr. MacGregor? What stairs was she found at the bottom of?"

"What?" There was that weird blankness again, like MacGregor wasn't even there. "It was an awful thing."

Will tightened the shot on MacGregor.

"Yes, yes. Very awful. Where did they find your grandmother, Mr. MacGregor? What's at the bottom of the basement stairs?" Blaine spoke clearly and slowly.

A book flew off the shelf as soon as MacGregor opened his mouth and slammed into the side of his head. His eyes rolled up into his head, and he collapsed.

"Holy fuck!" Will kept filming, but only because Flynn and Blaine and Jason had jumped in to help MacGregor. He wasn't such a jerk that he'd have left the guy knocked out on the floor. No matter how tempting it might be.

"Shit! Someone run to the kitchen and grab a cold cloth." Flynn barked out the order.

Darnell sprinted off. Will kept filming; he knew there was nothing constructive he could do at that moment.

Flynn took off his sweater, folded it, and put it beneath MacGregor's head. Blaine put his hand on MacGregor's chest as if to make sure he was still breathing.

"Jesus. Did you see that?" Jason asked. "Something doesn't want us going down into that basement—

something not nice either. You think there's two entities here—one good and one bad?"

Blaine snorted. "In a place this big and this old? There could be tons."

They all looked at Blaine.

"Seriously? Do you really think there could be not only more than one but a bunch?" Jason asked.

"I don't know. I know we're going to have to get into that basement at some point," Blaine said. "That's clear to everyone, not just me, right?"

Will agreed along with the rest. "Yeah. We might have to do it when he's not around, though. He could get killed if something else beans him in the head like that." Was it even safe for the guy to be in the house at all? "You think he should check into a hotel or something?"

"Do you think it'll let him out?" Darnell asked, arriving back with a wet rag in his hands. "Do you think it'll let us out this time?"

Will swallowed. He was a muscular, tough guy, but this was kind of freaky, and he had to admit to being nervous—to himself at least. This was more than them exploring some potentially haunted building trying to find ghosts. Something malicious was going on here.

Jason put the cloth on MacGregor's forehead. "Come on, man. Wake up. Wake up."

"We gonna take him to the hospital if he doesn't?" Will asked. Because this was fucked up. Like, really.

"Yeah, we'll need to." Jason patted MacGregor's cheeks.

"Damn. What hit me?"

"Charles Dickens's *Bleak House*." Will swung the camera over to where the book lay on the floor. Damn, that was a thick book.

MacGregor wrinkled his nose. "Oh. I never liked that one."

"Nobody liked that one. Especially when it hits them in the head. Come on, MacGregor, wake up." Will wasn't sure the guy was totally with them yet.

"I'm awake. Let me sit up. Damn, that throbs." Payne pulled himself up and sat there on the floor, leaning against one of the chairs. He blinked a few times. Frankly, he still looked out of it—in Will's decidedly nonmedical opinion.

"Let's get you to the hospital," Jason suggested.

"No. No, it happens. What did I say to piss it off this time?"

"It happens? Like, this isn't the first time?" Will shook his head. That shit was messed up. Just accepting it as a matter of course was even more messed up. "You didn't say anything." He was starting to think MacGregor was crazy, living in a house with ghosts that were clearly not friendly.

"Yeah." Jason tried to examine the cut and darkening bump on MacGregor's forehead. "I asked you about the basement stairs, and boom, you'd been taken out by Dickens. I suppose we should be grateful it wasn't a compendium."

"Do you have a first aid kit?" Darnell asked.

"I know there's one somewhere. It's not worth looking for now. I'm okay."

Darnell frowned. "But—"

MacGregor waved a hand in the air. "Don't stress it. Are you… do I need to get beds made up for you? Do you spend the night?"

"I'm thinking you should come stay with us," Jason suggested. "We all need to get out of this house, do some more research, and come back tomorrow with clear heads. I'm sure we can find you a bed with one of us."

"I've got a pull-out couch," Will admitted.

"Oh, I don't want to put anyone out. That seems unkind."

"Leaving you here seems unkind," Will countered. Big, renovated, sprawling, and fucking creepy. He caught sight of the lump on MacGregor's head. And dangerous.

MacGregor went bright pink, but Will thought he looked pleased.

"Come on. Let's go buy you a cup of coffee and talk about our next steps," Jason suggested.

"I could use a cup of coffee," MacGregor admitted. "Yeah. And maybe a bite of something sweet."

"Perfect, there's the diner on Swanson that'll still be open and have exactly what we're looking for." Jason sounded pleased with MacGregor's decision.

The man nodded and winced slightly, putting his hand to his head for a moment. "I'd like that. A nice little outing."

"All right, let's go." Jason made ushering motions toward the front of the house.

"You want me to keep filming?" Will asked, wondering if the door was going to open for them this time.

"Yep. We'll need establishing shots and whatnot. I think it'll work well to have them be from our first outing here."

"Sure thing, Jase." Will couldn't help but wonder, though, if Jason was thinking along the same lines as him. If they got some resistance when they tried to walk out the door, he wanted *that* documented.

MacGregor grabbed a windbreaker and his wallet and keys, then headed to the door, a look of determination on his face. Looked like MacGregor wasn't a hundred percent sure they were going to be allowed out either.

The rest of them followed MacGregor, and Will made sure to get a shot of everyone's face before they actually got to the door. They all exhibited pretty much full-on curiosity, though Blaine had that slightly out of it look he got whenever something was communicating with him… or trying to. Once Will had filmed all the teams' facial expressions, he panned the camera back to MacGregor.

MacGregor's lips tightened, and his mouth moved, the man saying something before he reached for the door and yanked at it. The door opened easily—so easily in fact that MacGregor almost went flying back against the wall. At the same time, there was an expression of relief on MacGregor's face, and as soon as he'd steadied himself, he went through the door like the hounds of hell were chasing him.

Will and the team headed out more sedately, and MacGregor pulled the door closed behind them and locked it. Will had to wonder if the lock was even necessary. Anyone idiotic enough to try and break into the place would be in for a rude awakening when they were either beaned in the head by a book or locked in.

MacGregor double-checked the door handle before clearing his throat. "Okay. Coffee. Pie. I'll follow you."

"You got it." Jason and the others headed toward the van.

Will finally turned the camera off and stowed it as they all climbed in. He started the engine and pulled onto the road to head toward the diner without checking to see if MacGregor was behind them or not. The guy knew where they were going, right?

"So," Jason began. "What do you think, Blaine?"

"I think he's in trouble. I think the fact that he could have this happen and never blink? I mean the guy got knocked out by a flying book and said 'these things happen.' That's weird, guys. Intense. He needs help. Something is working on him. And well-intentioned or not, that kind of thing is going to affect you."

"There's more than one ghost, though, isn't there?" Jason asked. "I mean, it felt like there was something positive as well as negative going on there."

"That's sort of my thought—that Payne's caught in the middle of a fight that isn't his." Blaine leaned against Flynn. "Ghosts can be good and bad, but this really felt like two different things."

"That sounds sucky." Will checked the rearview to see if MacGregor's headlights were there. They were. The guy drove a simple dark SUV. Will was pretty sure it was a BMW or some other luxury vehicle.

"You think the meanness comes out because he's gay?" Will asked. Though really, wouldn't it just be trying to drive him away if that was the case? He supposed if it was a relative, they could be upset about having someone gay in the family….

"What's with you and the whole mean thing, Will?" Jason asked. "He's been perfectly decent."

"I meant on the part of the ghosts, butthead." Although he supposed he deserved the accusation. He hadn't been overly friendly, and he couldn't explain why. MacGregor had rubbed him wrong on first sight.

"Oh." Jason turned bright pink. "Maybe? Blaine?"

"I can't help. I've got nothing on that, guys. Sorry."

"It was just a thought," Will said. "Given it seems these are old-soul entities, right?" The world had changed a lot since MacGregor's grandmother had died.

Blaine nodded. "I can agree that they've been there a long time. And that we're talking more than one ghost."

"Makes sense to me," Darnell said. "I mean, that house is… wow."

"Yeah," Will agreed. "Hell, we've been driving past it for years wondering what kind of ghosts it might be harboring. It's kind of cool we're getting to go through it now." It would have been cooler if there weren't bad stuff there, but they'd seen the general history—you couldn't expect happy ghosts coming out of something like that.

"It would be nicer if the owner wasn't caught up in it like he is," Jason pointed out.

"Yeah, yeah. Honestly, I don't have anything against him," Will told the guys. He had no clue why he'd taken such a dislike to MacGregor; after all, he didn't even know the guy.

"You think the ghosts were affecting you, man?" Jason asked.

Oh God. Will hadn't even considered that, and the thought of it sent a shiver through him. "I don't know." It certainly wasn't like him to be as big an ass as he'd been, especially without reason. He was a nice guy.

"Maybe…. Maybe we should keep you out of the house," Jason suggested softly.

He turned to glare at Jason. "Really? I apologized to the man." He was the cameraman for fuck's sake. He was a part of the team, and he was not going to wait out in the van like some naughty kid in a time-out.

"I meant if the spirits were messing with you, it might be better for you to stay out of their way, buttmunch."

"We never tell Blaine he can't go somewhere when they start messing with him. Besides, now that I know it might be a possibility, I'll be on my guard against them." Although he wasn't sure exactly how to do that if he was honest. He hadn't felt like he'd been… taken over or anything. He hadn't noticed any outside influence at all.

Maybe he'd talk privately to Blaine later on, see what he could do to keep from being influenced by anything malevolent. Sage and salt in his underwear, maybe, although that would chafe. A little chafing was probably worth not having a spirit using him, though. Just the idea of having a spirit using him made him want to gag. If that's what it had been. He guessed it was a better option than the idea that he'd just been a fucking asshole for no reason, though.

He pulled into the parking lot of the Silver Flyer Diner. He needed a beer. Or two.

MacGregor pulled in next to them, the man weirdly dapper with his neatly trimmed dark beard and his little round glasses. He looked almost old-fashioned. Like he belonged to the era when the MacGregor house had been in its heyday.

Now, was that the guy's style, or was it because of the house? Of course, MacGregor *was* a librarian. That didn't lend itself to modern, did it? Will probably wasn't the right person to start interrogating MacGregor over his choice of clothing, though, given the circumstances.

He gave MacGregor a nod, trying to make up for his earlier jerkitude.

MacGregor came over to them, offering everyone a shy smile. "Hey."

"Hey. I'm thinking a greasy burger and a beer instead of coffee and sweets. Anyone else hungry?" Will asked. Because now that they were here, his stomach was definitely more interested in an actual meal than some snack.

Blaine cheered. "We're always hungry!"

Will laughed as they went in and all piled into a large booth. As luck would have it, he was at the wall end of one bench seat with MacGregor squished up next to him and Darnell in the aisle in the last seat.

"Sorry!" MacGregor pulled in, clearly trying to take up less room.

Okay, it looked like he had been that big of an asshole. "Not your fault, dude. We can blame Darnell on the end there."

Darnell shot him the bird, and he laughed. MacGregor smiled, so Will did the same. It was easier, somehow, to relax here at the diner. Maybe it was the warm lighting and the smell of coffee, sugar, and fried things.

The waitress came, and they all followed Will's example, ordering beer. Jason asked for a pound of wings for the table too. Will figured he'd order his burger when she came back with their drinks. Now that they were sitting here, hungry had turned into starving, and he was eager for that burger.

"How long have you guys been working together? How did you meet?" MacGregor was probably just making conversation, but he did seem genuinely interested.

"Flynn joined us last year, but it's almost six years for the rest of us. Blaine and I have been friends forever." Jason smiled at Blaine. "Darnell and Will we've known since high school. It turned out we all believed to some degree, and we were all interested in ghost hunting."

"Wow. That's cool. Do you want a TV show? Is that the goal?"

"It has been." Jason shrugged. "And we got a show on an episode-by-episode basis after we had quite the experience with this abandoned hospital. But the last three 'episodes' have seen us debunking supposed hauntings, and the powers that be don't think that makes terribly good TV."

They weren't gonna lie, though. Will and the others agreed on that. They all knew ghosts really did exist and any pretending they did would only hurt them in the long run. Tarnish their reputation as legitimate ghost hunters. No way were they risking their credibility for ratings.

They wanted to help people, they wanted to prove that ghosts were real, and they wanted to make a living doing it, if that was possible. Making shit up and pretending there were ghosts in a place where there weren't any would bite that dream in the ass, sooner or later.

"We haven't had too many jobs where we help an individual with their ghost problems, like we're doing with you. But it feels...." Jason paused, clearly searching for the right words.

"Feel like the right thing to do," Will suggested, surprised at himself. It was true, though.

Jason nodded. "Yes, exactly. Like it gives us a purpose other than 'ooh, TV,' you know?"

"I like that. I don't.... It's hard to be made fun of for what you do, you know?" There was a deep pain, a humiliation, in MacGregor's green eyes. That no doubt explained why he'd been so sensitive to Will's grouchy behavior.

"Well, we're not going to do that," Jason assured him. "To begin with, we believe you. In fact, we're worried about you in that house. There's stuff happening, and it's not all good."

MacGregor nodded slowly and swallowed hard. "My worry is that it's getting worse, you know? More intense."

"We felt that," Will told him. Hell, the damn door had been impossible to open. Not stuck, not stiff—impossible.

"Yeah, it was like you were in the middle of two different entities, and they were both trying to use you."

"I don't understand. Seriously. Use me to do what?" MacGregor looked worried behind the wire rims of his glasses.

They all looked to Blaine. This was his bailiwick.

"That's the sixty-four-thousand-dollar question here, isn't it? If ghosts could just tell you, it would be a lot easier."

"I guess so. Hell, I'd settle for them telling *you*."

"It would be nice if it were that easy, and maybe they will, but I sense there's something there that isn't going to make anything easy. You're feeling a lot better now that you're out of the house, aren't you?" Blaine asked.

"I always feel better out these days," MacGregor admitted.

Blaine nodded sagely. "I'm not surprised to hear that. You might consider moving until we figure this thing out."

"I can't. That's my house, you know?"

"Even if it's hurting you?" Blaine asked.

Will didn't get that, needing to stay in a place that was toxic, not even wanting to be out of it for a couple of days. Maybe MacGregor didn't even realize what was happening to him while he was there.

"I don't have anywhere else to go. Not really." MacGregor shrugged his shoulders. "And I've poured myself into it."

"What about a hotel? Or you could stay with one of us." Jason made the suggestion again.

"Maybe I'll find a hotel for the night. We'll see."

Will had a feeling MacGregor was saying that to get them off his back about it, but the minute he left here, he was going straight back to the house.

Jason looked satisfied with MacGregor's answer, though. "I think it would be healthy for you to have a night away from the place. We'll go back tomorrow during the day. Most spirits aren't as strong in the light."

Their waitress returned with their beers and a big plate of wings. "You guys want anything else?"

"Yes," Will nodded. "I'd like a bacon cheeseburger, please."

"With the pub chips?"

"Yeah, that works."

"Okay. Anyone else?" She looked around the table, and to Will's surprise, it was MacGregor who put in an order.

"I'd like chicken fingers with onion rings, please."

"I love onion rings," Will noted. He hadn't thought to ask for them. "Can you change my pub fries to onion rings?"

"Sure. Anyone else?" she asked again.

"I'm good with the wings. What about the rest of you?" Jason gave them the same glance the waitress had, and Will had to bite his lip to keep from smirking or laughing outright. That was Jason for you. Sometimes he couldn't leave his role as leader of the Supers at work.

"I'd like some fries, actually." Flynn nudged Blaine. "You can share with me if you want."

"Double up on them," Jason suggested. "We'll share all around. I know once they get here and there's all this food on the table, I'll want some. Oh, I'd like some ranch dressing, please."

"Got it. It shouldn't be very long."

Will noticed she didn't ask if anyone wanted anything else. He guessed they'd used up all their one-more-thing ration.

"Meanwhile we have wings." Will grabbed one and dunked it into the pot of sour cream, then put almost the whole thing in his mouth and pulled the flesh off the bone. Damn, they were nice and hot.

"Impressive." MacGregor chuckled, green eyes sparkling at Will.

He chewed and swallowed. "The trick is to get the right end in your mouth, and it peels right off." It helped if you had a big mouth and weren't afraid to use it in public. And all that put together sounded way dirtier than any of it was.

"I…." MacGregor shook his head. "I got nothing. Absolutely nothing."

Will shrugged. "That's the trick. Like, for real." He hadn't been trying to be sexual or pull off innuendo or anything. Even though it had sort of turned out that way in the end. He grabbed another wing, dipped it in the sour cream, and ate it the same way he had the first.

"Wow." MacGregor shook his head but smiled at him. So Will figured it wasn't an insult or anything.

"It's a gift." He winked at MacGregor before licking his fingers. He'd wait until everyone had taken at least one wing before he grabbed his third. He was starving—sue him.

MacGregor nibbled on a wing, so careful. Okay, that was cute.

Will wondered if the guy ate everything delicately like that. Not him; he was a chow-down-and-demolish-his-food kind of guy. As evidenced by his one mouthful wing-stripping technique.

He hid his grin in his beer glass.

Jason smiled. "So tell us about you, Payne. What do you like to do?"

"I'm a librarian. I love books. I mean, I collect all sorts. I work from home these days, doing information collection. It's fascinating—the way that the old-school skills and the tech skills have melded."

"So like, full-time research?" Will couldn't imagine. They did research on the places they visited, of course, but that was fun and didn't really count.

"Research, organizing what information there is, dealing with making the information readable and accessible."

"You working on any particular subject?" Flynn asked, using a knife and fork to pull the meat from his wing. Who did that? It was kind of morbidly fascinating.

"Right now I'm curating information about medical history—saving the books for the sake of history. You can't risk leaving them lying around and having patrons believing the information's current, you know?"

"Do people really look at those old books as if that's accurate medical information they should follow?" Will always thought people in general were stupid, and this kind of confirmed it.

"Well, the thing is that even a few years can make a difference, right?"

"Yeah, I suppose. But with the internet, there's always going to be that information out there, whether it's out of date or not. Even if it's like, the worst advice ever, it still exists. It still looks right." A lot of people preferred self-diagnosing to going to the doctor, though.

"That's what I'm doing—trying to clarify so that there's less confusion." MacGregor shrugged. "I know that not everyone thinks it's worthwhile, but it's important."

"Good for you. It's good to have something to do that you feel is important." Like them and the ghost hunting. He fucking loved that stuff, and it mattered way more than delivering pizzas.

"I guess so, yes." Payne shrugged. "I'm sure your lives are more interesting than mine. Tell me about your exploits."

"Grass is always greener?" Flynn suggested.

Will laughed. "I gotta admit that I think our job is more interesting than MacGregor's. Sorry man, but it sounds really dry to me."

MacGregor nodded toward him with a distant smile and turned to look at Jason as he started telling stories. Then Blaine joined in, filling up the quiet.

Will added a detail here and there, all the while devouring wings. He felt guilty for a second as he was eating the lion's share, but he figured if the others wanted some, they could totally have some. He wasn't stopping them. He was even hungrier than he'd realized, though, because he totally still had room for his burger and onion rings when the waitress came back with plates full of food.

MacGregor ate very little—a couple of rings, one chicken strip—while listening to them silently, letting them all chatter. Will couldn't tell if MacGregor was actually paying attention or off in his own world.

Will finished his meal and sat back with a happy sigh. He grabbed his beer and took a deep drink, feeling so much better now, more like himself.

"So what happens next? Will you want to come back later?" MacGregor asked.

Jason answered for them. "We make sure you get checked into a hotel, and then we'll all go back tomorrow."

"When it's day," Will added firmly. Fewer things went bump in the light.

"I can deal. Seriously. I'll have to go get my laptop and chargers. Clothes. What time tomorrow?"

"We can go with you," Jason suggested. "Like I said, we want to make sure you get settled in your hotel okay."

"Nonsense. I'm a grown man, and you guys have better things to do than babysit me. I'll be fine."

"Don't be stubborn, MacGregor. It's all part of the service." Will drank the rest of his beer. "It's late enough you probably don't even need the laptop and shit. We could drop you off at the hotel and pick you up in the morning, avoid the house altogether."

"Do you mind letting me out, Darnell? I need to hit the head." Darnell slid over and let MacGregor out. "Thanks, man."

Will peered at the guys once MacGregor had left. "I didn't do anything."

"You really don't like him, huh?" Blaine asked.

"What? I didn't do anything but suggest the guy stay out of the house that's doing shit to him!" Honestly that hadn't been mean at all.

"You're just so gruff. Does he remind you of someone or something?"

Will hated when Blaine seemed so concerned. Especially if it was aimed at him. "I'm just being me. He doesn't remind me of anyone." Yeah, he'd been a bit of an ass at the beginning. He could see that now, and he was putting that down to being hungry. But he'd been totally normal since then and definitely hadn't been rude or assholeish since getting to the restaurant. Right? Dammit, now he was questioning himself, and that really would make him growly. Or, pardon him, gruff.

"Okay. Maybe we're all just sensitive." Blaine smiled at him, letting him know Blaine was willing to let it go.

"I will try to be extra gentle around him from now on, okay?" He rolled his eyes.

"Such a good boy." Darnell patted his leg.

"Fuck off, butthead." He bumped shoulders with Darnell, no heat behind his words.

MacGregor returned, and Will managed a wide smile. See him. See him be Mr. Nice Guy.

"I'm going to head out. I've paid the bill. I'll see you all tomorrow morning at the house."

"You didn't have to do that," protested Jason. "We're not on the clock."

"It was my pleasure. You guys have a good one. Night." And just like that, MacGregor was heading out the door.

"You think he's going to the hotel?" Jason asked.

Will snorted. "Nope. Not for a second."

"I think Will's right. I'm worried about what state he's going to be in when we meet him there tomorrow." Blaine sighed, and Flynn rubbed his back.

"Nothing you can do, love. We warned him."

"More than once," Will noted. "You can lead a horse to water, but you can't make him drink."

"He's been dealing with it a long time, you know. Maybe he doesn't have anywhere else to go." Darnell shrugged. "Maybe he doesn't know what to do."

"We said hotel. That's a place to go." Will sighed. He didn't think he was being unreasonable. He probably should shut up, though. "Anyway. We should do some more digging into the family and the house itself, eh? So we're better equipped in the morning?"

"Yeah." Jason nodded. "Yeah, that's a good idea. Hopefully he's there tomorrow, waiting for us."

It was going to be a hell of a short job if MacGregor wasn't. Will wasn't entirely sure which way he was hoping it would go.

Chapter Five

PAYNE went home feeling as stupid as a man could feel. It was obvious that these guys were... oh, he didn't know. He had no clue where his thoughts had been going. Maybe that they were good friends. Tight.

It didn't matter anyway.

He was just a loser librarian, all by himself in a great big fancy house. Maybe he ought to do some more research himself. He knew the history of course, but he'd never delved too deeply. It had him frowning. He'd meant to. More than once he'd been in the process of digging for more information, but something had always come up.

He went into the library, determined to do some more digging. There were books all over the floor, as if someone had walked through the room and dragged their arms along the shelves, sending the books tumbling. He sighed and picked up the mess of books, carefully dusting each one off and putting them back on the shelf where they belonged.

He was getting used to this kind of thing. Maybe he should learn to live with it. Maybe if he did, it would ease up.

He grabbed his laptop, poured himself a glass of brandy—he noticed the ghost had never tossed the decanter and spilled it; at least it had good taste—and settled into his chair to get some work done.

He woke up to a banging on the door, the sunlight pouring in the window. "Hold up! Coming!"

The banging continued. "Come on, MacGregor! We're going to break the door down if you don't answer right now!"

"Coming!" He stumbled through the house, still feeling fuzzy from sleep, and opened the front door. "Sorry, I fell asleep."

"Oh, thank God." Jason tugged him outside. "Are you okay? We've been ringing and knocking for fifteen minutes."

He frowned. Surely not for fifteen minutes. They were exaggerating. "I worked all night after I picked up the books."

"Picked up what books? Jason asked, keeping him on the veranda instead of going inside with him.

"There were dozens on the floor. Three shelves worth."

"Someone had a temper tantrum," said Will.

"Yeah, not me." He chuckled. "I just clean it up."

"Does that kind of thing happen a lot?" Jason asked. They still weren't going in.

"All the time. I need a cup of coffee." And to brush his damn teeth.

Darnell offered him a tray with four coffees on it. "Take your pick."

"You got one for me? Thank you." Oh, that was more than decent.

"Of course we did." Jason looked at the others. "We good to go in?"

"Come on. If they bother you, I'll threaten to burn the place down." He was too tired and sore to feel threatened right now. He was tired to the bone of the constant drama from something that wasn't really there.

Will laughed, looking surprised.

"Let's hope it doesn't come down to actually burning the house down," murmured Blaine.

"At least there's insurance, one way or the other." Although he didn't know if the insurance would pay if they thought he'd actually done it. If he did decide to go through with it, he'd have to look into it so he didn't get caught. God, was he actually thinking this?

"We're going to figure this out before it comes to that," Jason assured him. "Let's do this."

Will hefted the camera, and Jason made an "after you" motion.

He led them into the kitchen and doctored his coffee with a shot of cream. He drank deep, letting the heat and sweet soothe him. The caffeine worked its magic too, making him feel more awake.

"Day two at the MacGregor mansion. We're starting in the kitchen again," Blaine began as Will did a panorama of the kitchen. "Payne?"

"Yeah?"

"Were all the bowls upside down and stacked like that last night?"

He looked over at the glass front cabinets and, sure enough, all the bowls were on their rims and balanced instead of right side up and nested together.

"Holy fuck." Will moved in, panning the camera across the cupboards. "It wasn't like this when we were here yesterday. I've got the footage to prove it too."

"Yeah. I'll fix it in a little while." Asshole. Why did he have an asshole ghost? Or asshole ghosts as the case could well be.

"Actually, if you don't mind, I'd like to see what happens if you fix it now." Blaine pointed at the camera. "To see what happens and document it."

"Oh. Okay." Then he was going upstairs and changing clothes. Maybe taking a shower. He didn't need to be here while they played rearrange his cupboards and shelves with the ghost, did he?

"Mr. MacGregor is going to set his bowls back the way he usually keeps them," Blaine narrated, as Will filmed.

He put the bowls back together, cursing the ghost under his breath. One of the bowls vibrated, knocking against the others. "Stop it!" he snapped.

Something whipped the bowl in his hand away from him and threw it against the wall on the other side of the room, where it shattered.

"Oh, for fuck's sake!" He was tired and fed up, and he didn't want to play anymore.

Another bowl whipped across the room, the entire group of ghost hunters ducking as it sailed past them.

"Stop it! You motherfucker! These are mine!" He slammed the cabinets closed and held them shut.

Flynn moved to help him, and Jason held his hand out. "No! Not this time. We'll get involved with the next incident, but we need a baseline."

Payne thought this was incredibly unfair. He needed help. He needed support. He did not need the five of them standing there staring at him as the ghost tried to get rid of all his dishes. Maybe it didn't approve of his taste.

The dishes all rattled louder, the sound building as the cupboard doors pushed hard against him. Then all of a sudden it stopped. Just like that. One minute it was loud and strong and chaotic, and the next it was over. Like sunshine after a thunderstorm.

Will grunted. "Huh. All of a sudden the air is lighter."

"Yeah. Also yay." Payne didn't dare let go of the cupboard doors.

"You're feeling that too, Will?" Blaine asked.

"Yeah. How can I not? It's like suddenly being able to breathe again."

"Yeah. Yeah, this volley is over," Blaine said.

"Good deal." Payne stepped back from the cupboard, forcing himself not to shake. "I'm going to brush my teeth. I'll be back."

He was halfway down the hall before he realized they were following him. He didn't need company in the bathroom, right? They followed him all the way up the stairs, though, to his room, stopping just short of coming in with him.

"Can't be too careful," Jason murmured.

"I'll be fine." He hoped.

"We'll stay out here. But leave the bedroom door ajar and don't lock the bathroom door, okay?"

"Okay. The other bathrooms are along the hall if you have the need. They're all renovated."

"How many bathrooms does one hallway need?" Will asked.

He didn't answer. Obviously Will didn't care for him, or for his home. The house had seven bedrooms and eight baths—four on the second floor and four on the third. The first and attic didn't have any. He closed the bedroom door behind him. He wanted his privacy. Surely he'd be fine in his own room.

He brushed his teeth and washed up, using the time to shake off the last of the fuzziness from having fallen asleep while he was working. Then he changed his clothes quickly. It didn't feel right to be still wearing yesterday's clothes. They were no longer clean, and they were rumpled, and he wasn't the kind of person who was comfortable like that.

The guys were waiting in the hall when he opened the door, all watching Blaine, who was facing the other way, his head cocked.

Payne wasn't sure he wanted to know. Hell, he was pretty sure he didn't want to know.

"Give us a minute," whispered Jason. "Blaine has something."

"Okay." He went back in the bedroom and closed the door, sat on the edge of his bed, hands folded together in front of him.

There was a knock, and Jason popped his head in. "I didn't mean you had to leave. Only that we were waiting on Blaine to do whatever it is he's going to do."

"No worries. I don't want to interrupt." He wasn't a part of their group, and he wasn't sure if he was supposed to be that involved, really. Half of him thought he should go away while they were doing their thing; the other half thought that this was his house, and he wasn't leaving it.

"We're totally cool with you being right there with us—this is your house, your ghost. We need you there."

God, no matter what he did, he was off-kilter with these guys. Had he always been so... awkward? Of course, now that he was working exclusively from home, he had no way of gauging how well he interacted with others, because he didn't have to anymore. Not in person, anyway.

Jason motioned for him to come back out to the hall and join them. "Blaine has sensed a couple of presences since we got here. The one downstairs with the bowls, but there's a different one here."

Definitely two ghosts? Did that make him an overachiever? "Is that good or bad?"

"We don't know yet, but it does lend credence to our theory that there are at least two different entities here, and we think they're warring. And you are caught in the middle."

"Go team me." He tried not to sigh, really he did. It was bad enough to have one ghost, though, and now they were telling him he had at least two.

"This isn't your fault," Will, of all people, told him.

"I hope not. I didn't have ghosts before."

"They came with the house," Flynn told him.

It was almost funny. It was like a very bad joke. Only it wasn't a joke—it was his life.

"Yeah. I need to check the library. I left my computer in there." He didn't like it when they… it… whatever threw books around, but if they got it into their heads to toss his computer, it would break, and he couldn't afford that.

"We'll come with you," Jason said easily. And the entire group followed him, Will filming as they went, Jason making remarks now and then.

"You get used to it," Blaine told him.

"What's that? The ghosts?" He could believe that. If it weren't for the bouts of violence, he wasn't sure he would have called anyone in to deal with it in the first place.

"The ghosts. The camera. The weirdness of it all."

"I hope not. I don't want it to last long enough for me to get used to." He'd hoped he could call these guys in, they'd film the house, they'd find the ghost, and they'd get it dealt with. And he'd imagined that might take a few hours, maybe a whole day or night. Now they were on their second day here, and he'd gone from a ghost to at least two.

Flynn laughed. "Good answer."

"Not that you guys aren't nice, but this is stressful, the haunting thing." The having people he didn't know not only in his house but in his space, watching him all the time.

"Yeah, I'm sorry. I was trying to keep things light. We're going to see you through this. We're a good team, and we may joke around and fool around, but this is what we do. We will figure this out, okay?"

"I don't mind. I'm not a fuddy-duddy. I'm just tired." Exhausted, really.

"Fuddy-duddy. What a great word." Flynn patted his back.

"I knows lots," he teased, trying to match the lighter tone.

"I bet they're all big ones too," Will said.

"Oh, I know a few short ones." Ass. Dick. Plebe. He had plenty of choice words for Will.

Jason laughed. "We all know the four-letter ones."

"Those come in handy."

Will chuckled. "They won't let us use them on TV, though."

"True. I'll try to watch my mouth." He peeked into the library, sighing at the sight of a row of books stacked neatly on the floor. He supposed the stacking was an improvement over them being flung all over the place.

"Okay." Blaine nodded and moved ahead of him, Will following with the camera. "Here we have a row of books, neatly stacked on the floor. This feels like the work of a separate entity from the one who was throwing bowls across the room in the kitchen. Payne MacGregor, the owner of the house, is going to check out the books, see if there's any significance to them."

"They're children's stories—*The Five Little Peppers*, *What Katy Did*, *Little Women*, all sorts." The entire Famous Five series and the Narnia books too. They'd been his grandmother's favorites.

"Do these particular children's stories mean anything to you?"

"They were Gram's. She loved them." His strongest memory of his grandmother was lying in bed while she sat in a chair, rocking slowly back and forth as she read to him every night when they visited. Some nights she'd read for hours before he fell asleep.

"That confirms what I've been thinking," Blaine said. "One of the entities here is your grandmother. She's trying to let you know she's here. And the nonthreatening and nonviolent rearrangement of the books leads me to think she doesn't mean you harm. In fact, she may be trying to warn you or look out for you. It would be natural for her to be stuck here with the house if she was actually murdered. Maybe she was pushed down the stairs rather than fell." Blaine touched the books, fingers lingering over them.

Payne shivered at the thought of his gramma being murdered. No way was he thinking about that. Bad enough that she'd died like she had.

"Now we need to figure out how to communicate with her—find out what she wants." Blaine made it sound so matter-of-fact, normal.

"Well, tell her I'll do my best to give it to her." At least he thought he would. He supposed it would depend on what she wanted.

"I imagine she just heard you," Blaine noted. "Now we need to figure out who this other entity—or entities—are."

"I'm going to… I don't know. Fix myself a bowl of cereal." He was peckish, and this whole situation was so bizarre.

"How about we go down to the basement, first," Jason suggested. "You can show us around."

He opened his mouth to answer, but when he took a breath, he found himself sitting in the kitchen with his coffee. He looked around at the guys who were all staring at him, camera pointed right at him. What the hell?

"Is that you, Payne? Are you back with us?" Jason asked.

"What? Of course it's me. Don't be ridiculous." He didn't understand what was happening. Why couldn't he remember coming to the kitchen? Or making himself coffee?

"You want to see the footage?" Will asked. "We've got ten minutes of you being a zombie and refusing to let us anywhere near the basement door."

"Stop fucking with me." Zombies weren't real.

"Nobody is fucking with you," Will growled and took the camera off his shoulder, fiddled with something, then turned it in front of Payne so he could see the screen. "Watch the playback."

"…show us around."

He saw himself—or someone who looked an awful lot like him—shake his head and suggest they stay where they were. When that didn't work and the guys insisted they move down the hall toward the basement, he simply refused to talk. He stood there, staring into space, his hands by his sides.

"All right, let's go get a cup of coffee, then. How does that sound?" The guys led the way, Will obviously staying behind to film as Payne finally followed them. The team stopped at the door to the basement, but he pushed past them and went to the kitchen, giving the basement door a wide berth as he passed it. The guys followed him into the kitchen, where he sat. He didn't budge as Darnell made the coffee and set it down in front of him. Which was where he was now. And he had no memory of what he'd just seen or how he'd gotten from the library to the kitchen.

"Sorry. I guess I'm more tired than I thought." That had to be the explanation.

"It's more than that," muttered Will.

"Will is right. We think the other entity is riding you. It's trying to keep you from going downstairs or letting any of us downstairs." Blaine looked toward the locked door to the basement. He seemed worried. "I think that might be where its power is."

"No one needs to go down there. It's dangerous." Payne couldn't emphasize that enough.

"Is that you, Payne?" Jason asked, crouching next to him and looking into his eyes.

"Of course it is. It's important, okay?"

"Okay. But how do you know it's important to stay away from the basement? How is it dangerous?"

God, they were so pushy about the whole basement thing. He didn't want to talk about it. He didn't want to think about it. It was best to leave it alone.

"Think about it," Flynn said. "You were happy to show us the rest of the house and tell us all about the renovation. Why this reticence about the basement?"

He shrugged. It was dirty down there, stinky, dangerous. He'd opened the door once, and the smell had been awful, the steps incredibly steep. He'd decided then and there not to go down and to buy a lock for the door so no one could accidently start down there and do a header like his grandmother had.

"There's a lot of history in the basements of these old places, isn't there?" Justin asked. "A lot of them had kitchens and the servants' rooms."

"There is. These places are wild."

"So why aren't you renovating down there too? Why not fix it up? I bet there's a huge hearth for cooking that would make a beautiful fireplace. There's a lot of space down there that you're missing out on."

"I don't know," he whispered. He just knew that he didn't want to go down there, and he didn't want to talk about it.

Jason's eyes suddenly went wide. "Oh, honey. Your nose is bleeding."

"What?" He put his hand to his nose and pulled it away to find his fingers covered in blood. "What the hell?"

"Dammit." Flynn pulled some tissues out of his pocket and handed them over. "That started the moment you gave a free answer on your own, not the answer the ghost wanted you to."

"You don't know that for sure," Jason insisted.

"Bullshit I don't." Flynn shook his head. "I dealt with this with Blaine." Both Flynn and Blaine shuddered, then held hands. "We can't pretend this isn't happening."

"Can someone hand me another Kleenex?" This wasn't some little trickle of blood; this was a bad nosebleed. He'd never had one so bad.

"I'm out," Flynn said.

Darnell looked around and grabbed him a couple of paper towels.

"I think... I think I want to go lie down." He didn't feel so good. He wasn't usually that squeamish about the sight of blood, but there seemed to be so much of it.

"Someone should go with you," Flynn suggested. "I don't think you should be alone right now." The rest of the guys nodded in agreement.

Payne stood up, finding himself extremely dizzy. He swayed as everything went out of focus, then fell into someone's arms, the world going black.

Chapter Six

WILL caught MacGregor as he fainted, and Jason rescued the camera before it could fall and smash into God knew how many pieces.

"What the fuck!" He hoisted MacGregor into his arms, carrying him like a child. The guy was surprisingly light. Clearly all those clothes hid a fairly trim frame.

"Take him to his bedroom," Jason told him. "And stay with him. Something has got a hold of him. Something not at all friendly."

Will grunted. "Wouldn't it be better if someone else stayed with him?" He wasn't exactly MacGregor's favorite person. By a long shot.

"You have him. Just take him and make sure he doesn't…." Jason shrugged. "I don't know, explode or whatever."

"While you guys do what?" Will growled, not expecting an answer. He didn't want to be sidelined. He began walking his burden up the stairs. Macgregor leaned into him, relaxed and boneless, totally unconscious.

He went into MacGregor's bedroom and turned to find the guys had trooped up after him. He rolled his eyes. "I didn't exactly need the escort, you know."

Jason was manning Will's camera. "We're trying to document everything, though. And I wanted to know if he woke up once you got him away from the basement door."

"Fair enough."

"I'm going to close the door. We're going to try the basement. You make sure MacGregor is okay and text me if he's not."

Will opened his mouth to complain, but Jason had already closed the door. Bastards. All of them.

MacGregor began to shiver in his arms, making soft little cries. Oh God. What the fuck? He held MacGregor close and made shushing noises. This was not his forte. "Come on, man, you don't want to be doing this. If you were awake you'd be as embarrassed as all fuck."

Will stroked MacGregor's hair, the strands surprisingly soft. Not a hair-product guy, then.

He sat on the bed, but instead of putting MacGregor down, he kept holding on. MacGregor sighed and leaned in hard, resting on him like they were friends. Hell, like they'd known each other way more than a day.

Will didn't know what the fuck was going on, and that made him grumpy. He wasn't sure why Jason had thought it would be a good idea for him of all people to be coddling MacGregor. This whole thing was crazy. Starting with MacGregor needing babysitting. Passing out from questions about a basement. That wasn't normal. Blaine was right. Something was working MacGregor, manipulating him.

"You've got a real bug up your ass about the basement, bud. I'm sure we're going to find something super scary is living down there that's going to freak us all out. I mean, that's a serious padlock on that door."

Or maybe it was just a basement. Maybe MacGregor was insane. It was totally possible.

Hell, for all he knew, MacGregor had spent the night rearranging the books and the dishes in the kitchen. He could have faked the rumbling cabinets by shaking them himself while pretending to hold them down. The flying dish... well... MacGregor was a smart guy. Will was sure he could have rigged something up to make a bowl or two shoot across the room.

Yeah, that was probably it. Nothing scary here. Just some pranks. A way for Mr. Librarian to get some attention. He'd bet that's what this was. Some smart, lonely guy coming up with an imaginative way to get attention. Get himself on TV. Will squeezed MacGregor against his chest, his thoughts all chasing each other as he worked to convince himself that was what was going on here.

Damn, it was quiet. Like, really quiet. He could barely hear any breathing sounds from MacGregor, though he checked, watching until he could make out the rise and fall of the man's chest. Why was he still holding MacGregor when the bed was right here? How stupid was he being right now? God, what was wrong with him?

He stood and turned, carefully set MacGregor down on the bed. Worry clutched at him suddenly, and he covered MacGregor with the blanket that had been folded at the foot of the bed as if that would protect him. Protect him from what, Will couldn't say.

And how long was MacGregor going to be out? Where the hell were the guys?

He reached out, shaking Payne gently. *Come on, man. Wake up.*

Seriously, this wasn't natural. He was going to text the guys, see if they thought it made sense to take Payne to the hospital.

He's still out take to hospital?

He sat on the edge of the bed, jiggling his leg as he waited for an answer. None came.

Hello?

He got up and paced around the room, peeking into the bathroom. It all looked very nice and normal. What was taking Jason so long to get back to him?

Poke. He waited a few more minutes then nudged Jason again. *Poke.*

The fuck? If they were going to ignore him, he was going to go downstairs and get them. He took one last look at Payne, then held his hand in front of the guy's mouth, only taking his next breath when he felt warm air against his palm. Okay, Payne was fine. Well, still unconscious, so not exactly fine, but alive at least.

Will went to the door, turned the handle, and pulled the door... *not* open. Frowning, Will tried again. Then again. He put his foot on the wall next to the door, turned the handle, and pulled as hard as he could. The fucker didn't budge.

Banging on the door with two fists, he called out, "Guys! Jason! Darnell! Blaine! Flynn! Come on, guys. This isn't funny."

He jiggled the handle, trying to see if the door was locked, dammit. Though why they'd lock him and Payne in, he didn't know. He leaned down and peered through the keyhole, expecting to find it blocked with the key.

What he didn't expect was a shiny black eye, full of malice, staring at him. He stumbled backward. "Shit! Fuck!"

Oh God. He sat on the bed and shook his head. Okay. Okay. He was letting his imagination get away from him. Seriously. An eye? Some malevolent thing trying to see in? He was losing it. Next thing he knew, he'd be the one passed out. He took a few breaths and went back to the door, walking as casually as possible. He grabbed the door handle in one hand and turned it, then tugged. And the fucking door still wouldn't budge. So that part was not his imagination.

He'd look through the keyhole again. What he'd thought was an eye was probably the bottom of the key. It was one of those old-fashioned locks that would take an equally old-fashioned key, and those had rounded ends. And as keyed up—pun not intended—as he was, thanks to the guys locking him in here and not answering his texts, he'd let his imagination get away from him.

Bending, he looked through the keyhole again. Fuck him raw, that was definitely a beady little eyeball, and it was definitely not a happy little eyeball. The iris, outlined in a thin oval of white, was so dark he couldn't distinguish the pupil. He stared for a moment longer, telling himself his mind was playing tricks on him. Then it blinked.

He fell back with a cry. "Fuck!"

Okay. Okay. He was not looking through that keyhole again. That had *not* been his imagination, and the eyeball had not been friendly—quite the opposite in fact. He didn't know what the fuck was going on, but he couldn't say he liked it.

He went back to the bed.

"Dude. Payne. You got to wake up." He started tapping Payne's cheeks. "This situation is fucked up, and you refusing to wake up is making it even more creepy. So just wake up." He hit Payne's cheeks a little harder, then pinched Payne's right hip.

"Ouch!" Payne sat up, cracking their foreheads together.

"Fuck!" Will stumbled back, his hand going to his head. Shit, that had hurt. Payne had a fucking hard head. Not that anyone would be surprised about that.

"Ow. Ow, ow, ow. Why'd you bang my head?" Payne glared at him, and as annoyed as he might be, he had nothing on the anger in the keyhole eye.

"I did not bang your head. You banged mine." Will hadn't moved—Payne was the one who'd rammed into him.

"I didn't either! How did I get in here?" Payne demanded.

"You fainted."

"I've never fainted before in my whole life." Payne looked affronted.

"Yeah, well, I think you had help." Help from some supernatural badass with a creepy eye, it seemed.

Payne folded his arms around his chest. "This is too weird, man. Seriously."

"I know. Kind of what we do, though, you know? The weird and crazy. Ghosts riding people, needing wrongs righted, and all that shit." They weren't that well versed in it, though, and this was creepier than the old hospital had been. And that was saying something.

"I haven't done anything wrong. Nothing serious. I mean, I stole a candy bar when I was six, but I took it back and apologized…." Payne looked lost.

"Hey, dude. This isn't even about you, you know? You're just the guy on hand. Possibly your grandmother's ghost is here specifically to protect you, but the evil mother who made you faint and who flung those bowls around? That one isn't because of anything you did. Blaine said it felt old." Will paced from the bed to the door and back to the bed. Should he mention the black beady eyes looking at him through the keyhole? Probably better not to. Payne was already on edge.

Payne looked around and frowned. "Where is everyone else?"

"I have no clue. They were going to go check out the basement while I stayed and made sure you were okay, passed out but not dead." And now not only were they ignoring his texts, but the door wouldn't open, and it was deathly quiet.

"Well, let's go see what they're doing. It's scary quiet." Oh good, Payne felt that too. So at least that part wasn't his imagination.

"Yeah, it has been for a while." He went over to the door to open it—he wasn't going to say it was stuck only to have it suddenly be fine because then he'd look like an idiot. Or a liar. He grabbed the door handle—yet again—then turned it and tugged it hard. Yeah, not lying. Not imagining it. It wouldn't open.

Payne groaned. "Not again. I was stuck in here two days once."

"I hope you stocked snacks after that happened." That's what Will would have done. He was going to ignore the part where Payne getting stuck in his room was starting to become a habit. Will wasn't sure he'd still be living here if he were in Payne's shoes.

Payne gave him a wicked smile. "You know it."

Score! He returned Payne's grin. "Yeah? What's on offer?"

"I've got chips, doughnuts, cookies, chocolate, beef jerky, and a bunch of Cokes."

"Oh, we can live for days on that." He looked around. He could use one of those Cokes and some doughnuts, especially if they were the little ones with the white powder. Those were one of his weaknesses. Where was Payne hiding his booty?

There was a big wooden chest at the foot of the bed and Payne leaned down to open it, revealing the food and drinks in there.

Will reached for a Coke, then stopped himself. "Is it okay if I help myself?"

"Of course. Please." Payne went to the door and tugged at the knob. "Let us out! Come on. We're in here." He was getting as much of an answer as Will had—none.

Will grabbed a bag of the doughnuts—which were indeed the little powdered-sugar ones—and one of the Cokes. He set them on the bedside table, then strode over to the door and pounded on it with his fists. "Jason! Come on, buddy!" Frankly, he was worried that something had happened to the guys. That made far more sense than them locking the door and ignoring him.

"They're out there," Payne assured him. "The construction workers who were here when it happened last time didn't hear me either."

"Was it this quiet? Were the construction workers down in the basement too?"

"I don't know. I don't remember. Well, not in the basement because I haven't had any work done down there. But one minute I was in the kitchen, and the next I woke up in here."

"You've got a real problem here." He was still honestly surprised that Payne was staying here under these circumstances.

"That's why I called you. I don't know what to do."

"Yeah. We'll get it figured out. Blaine's our secret weapon because he's the real deal. And the rest of us are pretty good at reading the instruments. If you'd let us go down to the...." It occurred to him that if the entity had them locked up here and was dealing with the rest of the team downstairs, maybe it wouldn't stop Payne from talking about the basement.

He offered the guy a Coke and broke the seal on his own. Then he opened the doughnuts and put the package on the bed so they could both reach them.

"So," he began casually. "What's the story with the basement?"

"My gramma fell down there. It's always been scary, you know? Always. I don't understand why, but none of us liked it. I can't remember ever actually going down there," Payne admitted.

"That fits in with the theory that this other entity is old." Will drank his Coke. This whole place felt off, strange. Like the situation at the hospital. Something was going on. Big-time.

"I guess? I hate this. It's unnatural."

Will couldn't disagree with that. "You've got to deal, though. I mean what other choice is there?" This thing clearly wasn't going to go away on its own, and it obviously had a beef with Payne, given all the flying dishes and fainting.

"Exactly. I'm not losing my inheritance, this house, because of ghosts. No way." Payne looked adamant. It was good to see he had the gumption to fight for what was his.

"Then fight it is. You've got the right guys behind you now. Or beneath you. I have no clue where they are."

For all he knew they'd fucking left. No, he knew better than that. They wouldn't do that to him. They wouldn't have locked the bedroom door either. Not only could it be dangerous, but they wouldn't treat him like a kid.

"They're here. Of course, they might not even remember to look for us," Payne noted.

He shot Payne a look. That was a horrifying thought. "Surely not. It's not like they're random workers, and I'm a part of the team. They wouldn't forget we exist."

"Right. Of course. Of course they're looking for you."

"They'd better be," he muttered. "They'd fucking better be." He went over to the door and banged on it with his fists again. "We're up here! Stuck!" Fucking doors. Fucking ghosts. Maybe he should ask Payne to look through the keyhole. Though he didn't figure the guy needed the creep factor. Payne already knew his house was haunted.

"I don't understand any of this. At least we have a bathroom, right?" Payne was clearly looking for the bright side. As a silver lining, it wasn't that shiny, but Payne was right, there were a myriad of ways in which it could be worse.

"Yes. Trust me, peeing in a soda can is way less fun than advertised." Between the little hole being not only exactly that—little—but also sharp, it wasn't really that much of an alternative.

"Is it advertised as fun?" Payne asked.

"What? No. That's the point—it isn't advertised as fun, and it's even less fun than that."

"I was... I'm sorry." Payne sighed. "I was trying to ease the tension."

"Oh." Oops? He was always sticking his foot in it with this man. "I guess I was too tense for a tension easer?"

"I guess. I've done this before. You're new."

"I might be new but I can recognize that it's pretty damn fucked up." He looked around. It was such a normal room. Nicely decorated, but still very normal. "It doesn't feel spooky in here. Although I did see that dark eye staring at me through the keyhole."

"A dark eye? Really?" Payne shuddered. "Creepy."

It said a lot about what the guy had been through that Payne believed him, just like that.

"Yeah, it was fucking creepy. And not natural." He sat on the bed again and rubbed the back of his head. Maybe now he felt a little bit the way Blaine often did. Although for the most part, Blaine was pretty okay with the things he saw and felt. Will was not okay with being locked in a room and seeing creepy eyes staring at him malevolently.

"Maybe we should cover the keyhole with a scarf?" Payne hadn't stopped looking at the lock since Will had mentioned the eye.

"You think it's still watching us?" Will wasn't sure why he was as creeped out as he was. This was what he did for a living. Of course it wasn't usually quite so... personal. And he was used to ghosts who didn't come with actual eyes.

"I don't know, but I don't want it to."

"Yeah, good point. You got a scarf up here? Or a T-shirt or something?" Well duh, it was the guy's bedroom, so of course there'd be something they could use.

"I do. Here." Payne pulled a gray, patterned scarf out of a drawer and handed it over.

Will pushed the material into the keyhole, doing it quickly so he didn't linger very long. He was worried about his finger being vulnerable. Which was insane— it had been an eye and not teeth, and surely there wasn't anything with an eye that size that could get its mouth into the keyhole.

"Okay, that feels better, right?" Payne asked.

"Yeah, it does." Will snorted because it was silly, but it was true. It was like now that whatever it was couldn't see into the room, they were safe.

Payne nodded. "Yeah. It really does."

"So… you got any board games or anything in here?" Will looked around as if asking about it would make the games suddenly appear.

"I have movies and cards. Either of those work?"

"You wanna watch a movie, then?" That would be easier than having to talk. He didn't know what to say to Payne—they'd started on such a wrong foot. Which was entirely down to him. He knew he was the one who'd been an uncalled-for asshat.

"Yeah, let's do the movie thing. Nothing scary, though."

Will chuckled. "What, not *The Shining* or *The Blair Witch Project*?" He was kidding, honestly. He didn't need anything scary to freak him out worse than he already was, thank you very much.

"No *Poltergeist* or *Paranormal Activity* either."

"Damn." He gave Payne a wink to show they were actually both on the same page. "You got anything bright and cheery?"

"Uh… *Moana*?"

"You're not serious." Though he supposed a Disney movie—cartoon at that—couldn't be anything but cheery. At the very least have a happy ending.

"I like Disney!"

"I haven't seen it, so at least it'll be something new." He grabbed some of the pillows and piled them to one side near the head of the bed, then sat against them. Not bad. He shifted this way and that, wriggled his ass a little, and was good.

Payne searched through a pile of movies, before finding what he was looking for and sticking it in the Blu-ray player.

Will supposed the guy wasn't bad looking, if you liked the nerdy type. Which he'd have to admit he did. And Payne was a fine example of a good-looking nerdy type.

Figures he'd be realizing that now. He frowned. Why hadn't he noticed earlier? That wasn't like him. It wasn't like he was a horndog, at least not most of the time, but he did usually notice a good-looking nerdy guy who crossed his path.

Payne had been a sneak attack.

And Will was staring. He only realized it when he found himself caught by Payne as the guy stood and turned.

Payne looked over one of his shoulders, then the other. "Tell me there's not, like, a demon on my back."

Will shook his head immediately. "God no." Had there been a demon on Payne's back he could actually see, at least a little screaming would have been involved. "You've got a great ass." Dammit, he'd said that out loud, hadn't he?

"Oh. Uh. Thank you. I mean, that's nice."

"Sorry. Inappropriate, I know." He shook his head. God, what was it about Payne that turned him into an idiot? At least now he wasn't being an idiot *and* an asshole.

"It's still nice to hear. Sometimes I wonder if I'm invisible."

"Well, you work on your own here at the house, right? All alone for all intents and purposes?" Will thought that kind of thing would drive him crazy. He didn't mind his own company now and then, but day in and day out he'd probably bore himself to death. He liked having friends to talk to, to hang out with.

"Yes. Telecommuting, the wave of the future. Ghosts, the… wave of the past?"

"Not if they're affecting you now they aren't." Will knew he didn't want to work in an office, but he couldn't imagine working from home alone all the time. Even if he was hanging out with people in the evening, he couldn't see how the days would be anything but a grind.

Payne sighed again. "I was making a joke. Trying to, anyway."

Damn, he'd done it again. "I'm sorry. Honestly."

"I know. I mean, it's not the time, right?"

"It's probably the perfect time for joking. Keep things light." They were trapped in Payne's room by a beady-eyed ghost or demon or whatever. Who knew what the right thing was?

Payne sat on the edge of the bed and curled his legs under him, ignoring the TV and Blu-ray remotes on the bedside table. "Tell me about how you got into this?"

Will was about to ask if Payne really wanted to talk when they could be watching a movie, then he thought better of it. Why not tell Payne about it—it would pass the time.

"Blaine, Jason, and I met in the seventh grade."

"You guys were just kids!"

"Yeah, we were. We thought we were on top of the world, though. And when Jason's dad bought him a video camera, we knew we were kings. Jason couldn't figure out how to work the thing, but I soon sussed it out and became our main cameraman."

"So is that what you went to school for?" Payne asked, rearranging the pillows on his side of the bed and leaning against them.

"Oh, I only went as far as high school. We were going to be the Ghostbusters for real." He grinned. They'd been so optimistic back then, so sure they were going to have a TV deal. So very young. At least they all loved what they were doing, even if the TV thing hadn't happened yet. "What about you? You went to college?" The guy had to have if he was an actual librarian, right?

"I did. I have two master's degrees."

"Two? That's a little bit greedy, isn't it?" He hoped Payne figured out he was teasing. They didn't have a good track record with that at the moment.

"Well, I used yours." Payne winked.

Oh, good one! "Touché. So were you always a nerd?"

"I've always loved books, yeah. I mean, I keep thinking I'll write a novel one day when I retire, but I love research. I love putting things in order." Payne became animated as he talked about his work.

Will was glad Payne hadn't taken the word *nerd* as an insult, because it hadn't been meant as one.

"That's cool. I mean so not my bag. Although if it's about ghost hot spots, I will do a lot of research and enjoy the reading, but for that to be my whole life…." He shook his head. Honestly, he didn't have the patience.

"I know it sounds boring, but it's very satisfying. To put a piece of information somewhere and know I can retrieve it whenever I need to."

"Sure, sure. And it's a good thing we all find different stuff interesting and fulfilling, or everybody would want the same jobs and there'd be nobody to do everything else."

"Right. Exactly." Okay, that was a sweet smile.

"You want another drink? Some beef jerky?" He could totally get up and raid Payne's stash some more.

Especially as they'd need munchies for the movie. Or at least he would. He didn't know Payne's movie snack of choice yet. His was actually popcorn with lots and lots of butter, but that wasn't on offer here.

"I'm good, thanks." Payne grinned over at him. "I'm sorry you're stuck here, but it's so much nicer to not be alone."

It must have really sucked to be alone for Payne to be this happy to be stuck in here with Will. Although honestly, he was being nice now. Hell, he was feeling much more like himself.

"All part of the service." He winked.

Payne chuckled. "Man, you got the rough assignment."

"I don't know. At least we're on this side of the door from where the scary eye is. The guys are on the same side as it is." And there still wasn't any noise outside of the room. What had happened to the others?

"Yeah. Yeah, I get it. None of the workers saw a demon, though, right?" Payne offered.

"Very true. I'm sure they'll be fine." This was their job after all.

"Did they bring... salt? Silver?"

"Uh. No. We believe in communication. Besides, demons aren't real." Only ghosts. But maybe ghosts who could be evil enough one might think they were demons. They did carry holy water with them, just in case.

"How do you know demons aren't real?" Payne asked.

"Because they aren't. I've never seen one. Never seen anything that couldn't be explained or wasn't a ghost. They aren't real. Nasty ghosts? Evil ghosts? Sure, but not demons." Will refused to believe demons were real, and that went double now that there was a ghost outside of the room who had creepy, beady eyes.

"Huh. Okay." Payne shrugged, smiled. "You're the authority."

"Yep. Now how about we watch this cartoon of yours and see if the antithesis of our ghost problem will release the door." Lots of cheer to counter the boo factor.

"I hope so. I really do." Payne reached out, squeezed his hand. "Thanks for being here."

He turned his hand around and linked their fingers together, squeezed back. "Ditto. I wouldn't want to be in this situation alone either."

They sat there holding on to each other's hands. It was weird and strange and oddly comforting.

Chapter Seven

PAYNE tried not to let on how worried he was, how scared he was, how much he wanted to just curl up in the center of the bed and hide. Given that Will wasn't staring him down, he must be doing okay. The movie was helping a little—what with all the songs and good overcoming evil. Will's hand wrapped around his helped as well. At least he wasn't alone this time.

The movie ended, and Will got up, stretched, and walked casually to the door. Payne pretended he hadn't noticed, that he didn't know what Will was doing and wasn't waiting for the results with bated breath. Will grabbed hold of the doorknob, turned it and tugged. Nothing happened. Growling, Will pulled harder and still the door didn't open. Damn. Looked like they were still stuck in here.

"Fucking thing," muttered Will.

"I tried taking the screws out of the hinges, but it didn't make a difference." The door was well and truly stuck closed.

"How did you get it to open last time?" Will asked.

Payne shrugged. "I didn't do anything. I just tried it at one point and it opened."

"No shit? That's crazy. This is crazy." Will grabbed his phone again and shook his head. "No fucking bars—no wonder I didn't get an answer to my texts earlier. Do you think it's the good ghost or the bad ghost that's locked us up in here?"

"I don't know how you'd know. I don't even know how you'd tell them apart."

"I have no idea. I guess it depends on what kind of shit is happening on the other side of the door. I mean, if it's bad stuff, maybe the good one locked us up in here to keep us safe. In which case I'm pissed for the guys. On the other hand, if it's the bad ghost, I'm not sure what they're trying to accomplish. I mean, we have food and entertainment, even a bathroom. Despite being stuck in here it doesn't feel malevolent, although that beady eye did, I can tell you that much. But it could be that the good ghost is protecting us from that thing? That would be something a grandmother would do, wouldn't it? Even if she was a ghost. Blaine's the one who can communicate with them, so he'd know better than me who's who. I'm just making guesses."

"I can't communicate with any of them." Communication in person wasn't his thing. Electronically? He was fine. Ghosts fell under the in-person column. Even if they weren't really people anymore.

"Nah, me neither. I'm just the cameraman, equipment manager, and sometime researcher. Blaine's the one who's got the gift."

"Oh, you said the research word. Be careful," Payne teased.

"Oops, did I turn you on?"

"Right, like you wouldn't just turn me down." He might find Will attractive, but he wasn't into being rejected.

"Turn you down for wh—oh! Right. Honestly, I meant it as a joke—a double entendre." Will tilted his head before shrugging. "And you never know."

Payne snorted and went to find another movie. What if he was stuck in here forever this time? It was good not to be trapped by himself this time, but he hadn't laid in that much food, and he and Will were making short work of it. Another movie or two and there'd hardly be anything left. If they got out—no, when they got out—he'd have to remember to restock. It had happened once before, so he wouldn't be surprised if it happened again. He didn't want to be caught without food in that case.

Will's voice broke through his thoughts. "Of course, I think it's more of a matter of you not being interested, eh?"

Seriously? Will was going to put that on him? He'd never had a chance to decide whether or not he found Will attractive. Which, for the record, he did, despite the fact that until they'd gotten locked up in here together, Will had been a growly jerk. "You've been really clear that I'm not... that you're not interested."

"I know I was an ass. I don't know why. You're totally my type, but from the moment we met...." Will frowned. "I don't know. It really wasn't like me. I'm the easygoing type."

"Maybe it's chemistry. It happens." People found people attractive all the time only to find out they had zero chemistry together.

"It's weird because now that we're locked in here, it's like I'm seeing you with new eyes. I can't explain it, but I wish we'd only just met."

"It's fear, right?" They only had each other to cling to, so Will's earlier ire at him had faded. Wasn't that it?

"You think I suddenly think you're hot because I'm scared?"

"You think I'm hot?" He wasn't fishing or anything. He was trying to figure out how this guy who'd been so mean could think he was hot.

"Yeah. Like I said, you're totally my type." Will shook, his entire body getting into the move. "It's like I'm seeing you for the first time. Ever since we got locked in here."

That made the whole "it's because we're in here" thing more logical. Which was too bad because he thought Will was hot too. Although maybe that also came from Payne's bedroom. Wouldn't that be a hoot—if they could have this whole relationship right here in this room that didn't exist anywhere else in the world?

Will interrupted his thoughts again. "Anyway, yes, you're hot."

Payne blinked at Will, then his face warmed. "Thanks?" What did you say to that? Especially if it might have been some magic in the room itself. How embarrassing if he said too much, only to find the attraction gone when—if—they got out.

"You're welcome. Do you mind if I have more food? It feels like we've been stuck in here for hours."

"I don't mind at all. It's here for emergencies." And God knew this was an emergency. Besides, it had been several hours at the least, depending on how long he'd been out before he woke up.

"You think we're going to be stuck here for two days like you were last time?" Will asked, opening a bag of chips.

"I hope not. Your guys will surely think of something before then." At least he hoped so. He hoped they weren't hurt or stuck somewhere themselves. There was no way to tell.

Will pursed his lips. "I'm not sure they even know there's a problem yet."

"I'm not either. I don't even know if time is really moving for them. None of the workers had missed me at all." Which either was because time moved at a different pace, Payne actually was invisible, or the workers simply hadn't noticed he wasn't around. Of course, the most likely of those three scenarios was the last one.

"Well, that's really fucked up." Will shook his head and had a few chips before continuing. "I guess we can watch another sing-along movie to keep our spirits up." Will's eyes went wide, and then he started to laugh. "Pun not intended, which is a shame because it was a great one."

Payne blinked; then he started laughing too. That really had been funny.

And wow. A few hours together and they hadn't killed each other or even snapped at each other, and Will was being civilized, complimentary even. Payne would almost say that he was having fun.

He put *The Secret Life of Pets* on this time, and they watched it, munching away at his store of chips and cracking open a couple more drinks.

"Another?" Payne asked when the credits came on.

"Sure."

"How about *The Emperor's New Groove*? It's an oldie but a goodie." And he hadn't seen it in a while.

"Oh, I know that one!" Will grinned. "Why have we even got that lever?"

Payne laughed. That wasn't the exact quote, but it was close enough, and he wasn't going to prove how big an animated movie geek he was by correcting Will.

"My favorite thing about that movie is that Kronk makes his own theme music." Will grabbed another soft drink.

Payne put the disc in the Blu-ray player and got it started, grabbing the bag of M&Ms as he returned to the bed. He was definitely going to need to restock.

When *The Emperor's New Groove* was over, Will got up to use the facilities. Payne had to admit, he felt less safe with Will on the other side of the bathroom door, which was crazy, but there it was. He cued up *Sing* while he waited for Will to come back.

What if Will didn't? What if he got stuck on the other side of the door so they were both locked in separate rooms? Would he be able to hear Will if he called out? The longer it took for Will to come back, the more he worried that they were indeed stuck each in their own room now, and the anxiety of it built like a weight on his chest.

Then the door opened, and Will came out and closed the door behind him. "I hope you don't need to go in the next few minutes. There's something evil in there, and it's got nothing to do with ghosts, but the fan should take care of it soon. If you know what I mean."

Payne laughed, but secretly he was relieved. He didn't know if he wanted to close that door between them again. "I've got another movie cued up. It's another animated."

He hoped Will didn't mind. He, for one, was appreciating the light tone.

"That's cool. They're nice and easy."

And not threatening or scary. But Will didn't say it, and neither did Payne. No matter how much they were both probably thinking it.

Before coming back to the bed, Will went to the door and tried it once again. It didn't open, and he shook his head. "Crazy. I mean, it's been a long time for them to not come and check on us."

Payne shrugged. He didn't know what to say.

Will joined him back on the bed, sitting back against the pillows. "At least you've got a comfortable bed and plenty of entertainment. The Cokes and munchies aren't bad either."

Payne was still simply grateful he wasn't trapped on his own again.

Will shifted slightly, and their shoulders touched. Like the hand-holding earlier, it was comforting.

This time during the movie, Will kept glancing at the door. Like now that he'd checked it and remembered it again, he couldn't let it go. About halfway through a song-and-dance number, he went over and tried the door once more. It didn't open, and Will sighed before returning to the bed, sitting close.

"I'm sorry. I could try to fall asleep. I even have some sleeping pills."

Will blinked at him. "How is that going to help us get out of here?"

"I don't know. I saw a horror show once where the doors opened when they knocked one of the characters out. So if we need a volunteer, I can do it."

"Well, you were passed out when I brought you up here and the door locked while you were still passed out.

I don't know if that means you being passed out makes a difference one way or the other, but I can tell you I'd rather be locked in here with you awake than not. That was freaky."

"Oh good. I really want to be awake." The idea of being out of it while this weirdness went on freaked him out a little, though he would take one for the team if it unlocked the door. Not that being stuck in here this time was all that bad. Will was good company.

"Awake it is." Will said the words decisively. "I'm not even going to offer to be unconscious. Not because of you but because of the ghosts."

"We'll keep each other company, right? Play cards." As clearly the movies were no longer holding Will's interest. Maybe Will just didn't appreciate singing pigs.

"Yeah. Play cards, watch bad movies, and eat you out of your treasure chest." Will leaned over to open the chest at the end of the bed, his T-shirt slipping up to expose his midriff.

Payne averted his eyes, trying not to look. This was not appropriate. Will seemed oblivious, shifting and stretching a little more, his ass turning toward Payne. How could Payne not look at that?

God, he was a perv. He'd hired these guys. They were his employees for Pete's sake.

Will brought up several chocolate bars and a box of Chex, along with two more Cokes. He handed one of the cans over. "Hey, you okay?"

"Huh? Yeah. Yeah, I'm great." *Just admiring your butt.* He hadn't said that out loud, had he? Will didn't appear in the least bit fazed, so he was guessing no, he hadn't. Thank God.

"Okay. You want the Coffee Crisp or the Aero bar? Or we could share and have half each."

"Let's share. I'm friendly that way."

Will chuckled, the sound wicked as hell. Then he split both bars and offered the halves to Payne to choose which ones he wanted. He took the larger of the Coffee Crisp pieces and left the slightly bigger of the Aero for Will.

"You're a coffee fan, eh?" Will took a crunchy bite of his half of the Coffee Crisp.

"How did you guess?" He grinned and winked. He loved tea too, and his Coke. He liked caffeine whatever form it came in. Though he wasn't very fond of energy drinks. When he needed one of those, he drank it despite the taste.

"You took the bigger half of the Coffee Crisp. And I think you've made at least a dozen coffees for us, and we've only been here twice." There was no heat behind Will's exaggeration. He was clearly teasing.

"Yeah, yeah. It's something to do with your hands when you're nervous, right?"

"You were nervous to meet us?" Will sounded surprised.

"God yes. What wasn't to be nervous of?"

"How come?" It seemed like a genuine question— Will much nicer now than he'd been when they'd first met. Less prickly and confrontational.

"Well, there's the whole 'you're crazy' part. That's the worst. More than that, there's the 'you're crazy and paying....'" He worried about what other people thought—it was one of the reasons why working from home was easier.

"Except we don't think you're crazy. We think you've got a couple of ghosts here, and they're very definitely playing tricks." Will pointed at the door. "That's not your imagination."

"No. And I swear, I didn't do anything to cause this." This was totally out of his control.

"Yeah, I didn't think you did. Nobody asks for a ghost. Well, except maybe Flynn, but that's a different story than what's going on here. When we did research on the house before coming, there was nothing confirmed about ghosts at all, only speculation. Looks like your family never shared what was going on here with you. With anyone, really."

"My mom wasn't interested in spending time with my gram, and once Dad was gone.... Everything changed." He guessed once his father wasn't in the picture anymore, his mom figured she didn't have to spend time with his side of the family.

Will tilted his head. "Did being here at the house bother her? You said that you'd had an imaginary friend here when you were little. Did she know about that?"

"Probably. I mean, I'm sure I talked about it."

"Maybe she knew there were ghosts here too, and she was trying to keep them away from you?"

"Does it work that way? That's sweet."

"Well, in my experience moms are fierce about their kids. I don't know if she knew about the ghosts or maybe had a bad feeling about the house. It's too bad we can't ask her. Oh damn, that sounded cold. I'm sorry for your loss and that she's not here anymore."

"Me too. She was a neat woman." Payne smiled, because she'd been his opposite—outgoing and warm and charismatic.

"It's your father's side that the house comes from, though, eh?"

"Yes. Yes, exactly." He finished the chocolate, the sugar and caffeine helping improve his demeanor.

"From what we read, Angus—your however many times great-grandfather who had the place built—was a beast and ran his workers into the ground."

"That seems to be pretty common, huh?" It sucked, but it had happened frequently back in the day. Things had changed a lot since the eighteenth century.

"Yeah, that's what we said. There were rumors it got pretty bad, though. Maybe the ghosts are related to that."

"Maybe. Do you think they want me to go?" He didn't have anywhere else to go. This was his, and he'd put so much into restoring it.

"I don't know. Someone is pissed, and someone is on your side. That's my feeling on it, anyway. Hell, maybe there's a dozen of them and they each have a different agenda. Who knows?"

"Maybe." God, that was a nauseating thought.

"Sorry." Will bumped their shoulders together. "That doesn't make it better, does it?"

"Not really. In fact, that's super scary." It had been hard enough thinking he was living with a ghost. Then it had been suggested there were two, and now Will was speculating on a bunch? He shivered.

"Yeah, sorry. I'm not even the one with the gift, so it's all speculation on my part. We'll have to quiz Blaine when we get rescued."

"Or when we rescue them." Payne wasn't ready to be the victim. Not yet.

"We'll have to get out of here first. You have anything we can use as tools? Maybe a saw or two?"

"I don't keep saws in the bedroom. I have a hammer and a couple of screwdrivers because I was fixing the drawers and putting new handles on them."

"Given the circumstances, maybe you should start. We could try using the hammer to put a hole in the door, though. Rescue ourselves and make sure the guys are okay." Will cracked his knuckles and gave the door an evil look.

"Have you tried the window? When I was stuck in here before, it was boarded up, but it isn't anymore. Maybe we can get their attention by screaming out of it."

"Duh, the window." Will rolled his eyes. "Why do something easy when you can do it the hard way—that'd be my motto a lot of the time. I can't believe I didn't even think of that." Will got up, went to the window, and pulled the curtains to the side. "Well, it's still boarded up. I can't remember ever seeing such a tight placement of the planks on a boarded-up window. *Ever.*"

Will tried the window, then moved the locking mechanism and tried again. Payne could almost feel Will's frustration when the damn thing didn't budge.

"I could try breaking it… but I'm not sure that matters with the wood behind it. It would still be a long shot that anyone would hear us."

"It wasn't boarded up before, Will. They took the planks down last week when they put in the glass." Payne felt a little sick. "Hell, there was light coming in here a minute ago. Before we mentioned it."

"You know, you're right." Will grabbed Payne's hand and held on. He frowned. "Although now that I'm thinking about it, it seems like it was lighter than it should have been as long as we've been in here." He shook his head and went on, "Anyway, I don't think we're going to be getting out on our own and rescuing anyone else, Payne. For some reason the house wants us in here. Like, really wants it." Will didn't look any happier than Payne felt about that.

"I'm sorry. I'm really sorry. I didn't mean for any of this to happen."

"You don't need to apologize. It's very clear this isn't your doing." Will took a breath, then grabbed on to Payne's shirt, tugged him close, and planted a kiss on his lips.

Payne's eyes went wide, utter shock surprising him. The kiss was warm and intense, filling him with an electric buzz. It felt good, better than good, even. Groaning, Will deepened the kiss, pushing his tongue into Payne's mouth.

What was this?

Payne gasped, letting Will in farther, deeper. Will pressed forward, and Payne wound up on his back on the mattress, Will leaning over him as the kisses continued. It went on and on, and he didn't stop it, didn't pull away or push at Will's muscled chest. In fact, he wrapped one hand around Will's hip and tugged him closer as he spread his other hand over Will's T-shirt, fondling those muscles through the thin material.

Shifting, Will moved against him, rubbing their bodies together as one kiss flowed into the next, Will utterly stealing his breath. Payne gasped, his body suddenly tight, hard. Will answered him with a moan, the noise filling his mouth, his lungs, and seeming to vibrate there.

God, he wanted. He wanted more. He needed this desperately.

Wait. Stop. Desperately? Stop. This couldn't be real.

He tore his lips from Will's, blinking up at the man, at the fierce passion he read in Will's face. "Is this real?"

"It feels fucking real. I want you, man." Will pushed against him again, letting him feel the drag of the thick cock pushing at the fly of Will's jeans.

Yeah, okay, but… "Why?"

"Huh?" Will kept rocking against him, clearly distracted by pleasure.

"I…." Payne wasn't sure what he was asking. "Why me? You didn't like me yesterday."

"I think that was the house. You're totally my type, and I want you. I've got to fucking have you. Right now, and—whoa." Will sat back and shook himself. "You *are* my type, and I think you're hot, but you're right. This desperation doesn't make sense. It can't be real."

"Yeah. Yeah, I mean, you… I want it, but…." He wanted it to be real. He didn't want to do this and find out later today or tomorrow that it had been the influence of the house that was responsible for this need.

"This sucks." Will sat again, then helped Payne upright and straightened his shirt. "Not you, but this whole might-not-be-real thing."

"Yeah. If… when we get out, if you still want to, though…." He didn't want to come off sounding slutty, but he thought—hoped—there might be something here worth exploring.

Will grinned, the expression both wicked and boyish at the same time. "Ditto."

"Oh, cool." He smoothed his shirt down, careful not to touch his cock. He didn't want to aggravate anything.

"If it means anything, I hope it's real." Will touched his hand, squeezed it.

"Me too. I haven't had good sex in a long time." Not that he only wanted sex from Will. He wasn't a one-night stand kind of guy.

"Well, that's a damn shame. We could always go ahead knowing it might be a one-shot deal. Let you get you your rocks off." It was a generous offer—although really, how many guys wouldn't want to get their rocks off, no strings attached—but Payne wanted more than that.

"No. No, I want…. I know it's old-fashioned, but I want someone to at least like me before I get into bed with them."

"I'm pretty sure I like you." Will scrubbed his face with his hands. "And I hate that I'm not completely sure. I hate that it feels like this house is controlling us."

"Yeah, it's creepy. I'd just leave, but I've sunk everything into it. All my savings."

"It's one of those things where on paper you're golden, but in actual liquid assets, you're less so, eh?" If Will had asked that question yesterday or this morning, it would have rankled. Now it didn't.

"Well, I do own this house, but I can't just leave it. So basically, yes."

"That's what I was trying to say. Can you tell I'm not Mr. Finance for the group?"

Payne chuckled softly. "I mean that I'm not allowed to sell it. The will states that it has to stay in the family." So even if he wanted to leave, he wouldn't be able to sell the place. He'd have to let someone else live there. If he could even find someone willing to rent it.

"Wow, that's kind of harsh. I mean, it could be an albatross. Especially with the ghosts it comes with."

"It's a beautiful albatross, though, and the bones are good." Even if Payne hadn't had the money to return it to its former glory, he would have moved in. Maybe fixed up his bedroom and the kitchen. Oh, and the library. Thank God he'd had the money, because even just one of those rooms would have been expensive, and thinking of it now, he couldn't decide which one he thought was more important.

Will made a face, scrunching his nose up. "I'm not sure I want to think about a place like this with bones. I mean, it's already creepy."

"Not always. There are times it's really pretty, this amazing big place." If he could get rid of the ghosts, or find a way to co-exist with them that didn't involve flying dishes or books, it would be the best home he could imagine.

"Hopefully we'll fix it so it's always pretty and amazing." Will said it like he believed it could happen.

"I hope so. I want it to be a jewel, something to be proud of." He wanted people to know the MacGregor house as a piece of history. He wasn't going to have anyone to leave it to, but if he could leave it as a museum or something, well, that would be quite the legacy.

"Well, its owner certainly is," Will told him with a warm smile.

"Is that weird? I don't think it's weird."

"That I think you're a jewel? I don't think it's weird either."

"Oh!" His cheeks went hot. "Thank you. Seriously, thank you."

Will sat back, looking happy at his response. Payne hadn't even considered that Will had been talking about him.

Will pointed at the TV. "How about we watch an action film or something. Pretend we're on a first date."

"I can get into that. A blind date." Payne held out his hand. "Hello, I'm Payne. Pleased to meet you."

Will shook his hand. "Will. Same. So, this is a pretty small theater, but it's intimate, and the snacks are great."

Payne played along happily. "Those are the best kind. It's hard to talk in a crowd."

"And people get so snarky when you talk during a movie."

"I know, right? When sometimes you need to make a comment." How could this be so fun?

"Exactly. And I mean, sometimes you have to stop and pause to count Thor's abs." Will licked his lips.

"Oh, a man after my own heart."

"Or at least after Thor's abs." Will gave him a wink. "Do you have any of the Thor movies—it would be a shame not to enjoy the abs we've been talking about."

"Any? All. Seriously. All." He found the first one and popped it in. These were on regular rotation.

"Perfect. So far, this is the best first date ever. I'll buy the snacks." Will dug into Payne's chest again, coming up with more chips, Cokes, and another bag of M&Ms, then sank back against the pillows.

"So far it is. It's the most fascinating first date on earth."

"Come sit. I saved this seat here just for you." Will patted the empty spot beside him.

"Thank you." He settled next to Will, that buzz of electricity hitting him again.

Will looked at him, and Payne could see in Will's eyes that Will had felt it too.

"Static, right?" Payne asked.

"If that's what you want to go with. I like to think of it as first-date electricity."

"Oh, that's a lovely thought." He hadn't thought Will could be so... sweet. So far even when he was being nice, Will seemed... tough.

"See? I'm not all rough and gruff—I can be romantic." Will linked their fingers together again.

"I'm not very rough, but there's something appealing about a gruff man." Look at him flirting, like you were supposed to do on a first date that was going well.

Will tilted his head. "Yeah? Because I'll own that there are times I can be gruff. Not assholey gruff like when we first met, but still. Don't talk to me before my morning coffee."

"How do you feel about pre-coffee kisses?" Because some things were good no matter when they happened.

"Kisses are good at any time of the day. Even pre-coffee." Will's words echoed Payne's thoughts nicely.

"Then we'll get along in the mornings."

Will gave him a suspicious look. "Are you a morning person?"

"God no. I work late at night. That's why I telecommute." He wasn't made for the whole nine-to-five gig.

"Thank God you're not a morning person. That's just not natural." Will actually shuddered.

Payne began to laugh, the sound almost shocking him. Okay, that was great. This was exactly what he'd needed.

Will looked pleased again. "Dude, you've got a great laugh."

"Thank you." God, he wanted another kiss. So badly.

Will kept staring at him, then he leaned in a little, looking at his lips now. Maybe Payne wasn't the only one wishing for a kiss. They held that pose for a minute, staring at each other's mouths.

The door flew open, the guys tumbling in. All four of them. "What the actual fuck?"

Payne's head turned so fast he almost gave himself whiplash. "Oh my God."

"Will! What are you doing?" Jason demanded.

Will jumped up and growled. "Waiting to get rescued. We've been locked in here for hours!"

"Hours? Bullshit. It's been twenty minutes." Jason sounded utterly shocked. "You were supposed to watch him, not paw him!"

Will blustered. "I was not pawing him! And it has too been hours. We watched God knows how many movies. Ate a zillion snacks. Spent ages trying to get out. Back me up here, Payne."

"It's true. We've watched four movies. Well, three and a half." They'd given up on *Sing* partway through. "We've tried to get out. We're not lying."

Jason stared at him and Will like they'd lost their minds.

"Did you guys have trouble getting in?" Will asked.

"No. We heard MacGregor laughing."

"That's because I'm funny as hell." Will gave Payne a wink.

Payne grinned over. "True story."

"What?" Jason looked bemused, like he couldn't understand at all what was going on.

Payne shrugged. "He makes me smile."

"Did you fall and hit your head?" Jason asked.

"How would I know? I was unconscious." He had no idea what had happened.

"Be nice," Will admonished Jason.

"What?" Jason looked utterly flummoxed. "Did you... seriously?"

Payne grinned at Will. It had been a weird date, but a good one. And it had helped make the time they'd been stuck go faster. Had it really only been twenty minutes outside of the room? Payne glanced at the window. Which was no longer boarded up, letting the daylight shine in. Okay, that was freaky as hell.

Will went over and put his arm around Jason's shoulders. "We were stuck in here for hours, we couldn't hear anything—even the damn window was boarded up. We made it work. Now what were you up to in the so-called twenty minutes before you came up here and informed us we're all on different time? Did you guys make it into the basement?" Will looked back at Payne as he asked the last question.

"No, we couldn't get the lock off. We came for permission to break the door."

Payne shook his head without even thinking; it was out of the question. "No. No, that's original to the house."

They all looked at him like he was crazy. And Will came over to him and put a hand on his shoulder.

"I know it freaks you out for some reason, but we're really going to need to get into the basement or you're going to be stuck with this scary-assed ghost who locks people in rooms for the rest of your life." Will rubbed his shoulders gently, fingers barely pushing in. The touch was a comfort, easing him.

Jason was still looking at the two of them like they'd lost their minds. Not just him either. The other three behind him seemed to think he and Will were behaving oddly too. Oh God, were they?

"Would you put your eyes back in your head?" Will kept massaging him. "We had nearly an entire day to kill, just the two of us stuck in this room."

"We had a lovely date, didn't we?" They'd had a... meeting of the minds.

"Yeah, we did."

"Date?" Blaine stepped in from around Jason. "Guys, I'm not sure you're yourselves."

"I'm just fine." Maybe he'd gone a little horny, but they had the sense to stop, give themselves time. "And so is Will."

"Twenty minutes ago you couldn't stand each other. Now you've been on a date?"

"First of all, we've been up here all day long," Will pointed out. "We've had lots of time to talk. We ironed shit out."

"And you're discounting that there might be ghost interference going on here?" Blaine asked.

"No. But you're discounting that the immediate dislike could have been ghost interference." Will had a very belligerent set to his shoulders.

"Can we all go down to the kitchen?" Payne suggested. "None of us want to be here, trapped." While in the end it had been fun with Will, there was not a lot of room for six adults, and they'd nearly polished off all his supplies.

Will agreed immediately. "Yeah, we've eaten most of your stash."

Once again, he and Will were on the same wavelength. "Right? We'll have to refill."

"Bring an ax," Will suggested.

Payne began to cackle, hooting with laughter. He was going to be the only person in the country who slept with an ax under the bed that wasn't to use against intruders. Instead he'd need it to get out.

Will's buddies stepped closer to each other. It was subtle, but it definitely happened.

He stopped laughing and looked at them. "What?"

"I'm not sure the two of you are okay. Let's go downstairs, eh?" Jason and the others backed out of the room, encouraging him and Will to follow.

He sighed softly. The first really positive thing to happen in weeks and no one was happy about it. Will rolled his eyes and fell into step with him. Well, not quite no one.

Will touched their shoulders together. "We were wondering if it was real or not."

"The intensity, yes, but not the laughter."

"No, I'm definitely a funny guy. I'm not giving that title up."

"You've both lost your minds," Darnell muttered. "I'm calling a priest."

Will shook his head. "We really are fine, you know?"

"Yeah. I think we really are." He wanted to reach out, touch Will's hand.

Instead, Will touched him, the faintest brush against the back of his hand. Yeah. Still electric. Cool.

Will glanced at him out of the corner of his eyes and gave him a little grin. Payne's lips quirked of their own accord, and he found himself fighting the giggles. He almost felt drunk on happiness. On Will.

Maybe it was heightened. Maybe it wasn't. So what? He deserved a little happiness, didn't he? Even if it was helped along. Even if it was fleeting.

They got down the stairs and as a group stopped in front of the basement door. Payne and Will were at the back of the group, or Payne would have gone on into the kitchen. He didn't want to be standing at that spot.

"Okay. We need to get into the basement," Jason said, looking right at him.

Payne shook his head. It was scary down there. He had to stay away. They all did.

"I know you don't want to, and you don't have to go down there. But it's clear there's something in the basement connected to everything that's been going on. So, we need to go down there and see." Jason spoke clearly and slowly.

Will's hand landed on the small of his back. "You won't be alone, you know? I promise."

He opened his mouth to say yes, just to get it over with, get it done, but the word wouldn't come out. Everything got fuzzy around the edges, the only solid thing was Will's hand on his back. He thought for a minute he was going to pass out again, only this time he could feel it happening.

Will kept touching, kept petting him. "Let's take him out and let him breathe, okay, guys?"

He could barely hear the words. It was like he was wrapped in cotton wool. The cool air hit him suddenly, and he gasped, shocked to discover they were outside.

"Hey. You really have to stop passing out, man." Will was holding him, cradling him against the strong chest.

He struggled for half a moment before he curled his fingers around Will's shoulders and held on. He shook his head. That didn't make any sense. "I passed out?"

"Little bit, yeah." Will rolled his eyes.

"You passed out last time we got pushy about the basement," Flynn noted.

Jason nodded. "And yesterday it seemed like you were possessed every time the subject came up. That makes us believe it's important for us to get down there."

"I'm not possessed. It's just a bad place." Talking about the basement made him really uncomfortable.

"We want to help you with that. Hell, that's what you're paying us for, right? We've got to get to the basement. No matter how hard whatever's down there fights us." Jason made a face. "Are you sure we can't break down the door?"

"Why don't we buy one of those lock cutting tools?" Will suggested. "Or hire someone to cut it off. Does that work, Payne?"

He nodded, even though he didn't want to. It did work—he didn't like it, but it covered all his objections, and he couldn't think of any other ones at the moment.

"That's a great idea, Will." Jason patted Will on the shoulder.

"Gee, thanks for sounding so surprised that I came up with a good idea, Jason."

Payne chuckled softly, and Will patted his ass.

Jason gave him and Will an eagle-eyed look. "You two are being super weird. I just thought you should know."

"You've said. Are you two dating?" Payne was going to kill Will if that was the case. Except maybe it was the house, so it wouldn't be his fault.

"Is who two dating?" Jason asked.

"You and Will. You seem very concerned that we're getting along." Not that he was jealous.

Jason snorted as he shook his head. "No. No, we are not dating. I'm just concerned about the fact that you guys hated each other on sight and twenty minutes in that room together and you're, well, flirting at the very least. I just think it should be noted that there's been a lot of unusual behavior going on when it comes to this house."

"You're right about that." Will looked back at the door. "Though frankly, the out of character stuff for me was my assholery when we first got here. You're not usually one to harp on stuff, Jason. Maybe you're being affected too."

"Maybe," Jason admitted. "This place is... wow. It's intense."

"So do we need to do another trip away to go over what we think, just to make sure none of us are being affected by the place?" Will asked.

"We could all come to the barn. All of us. Just for the rest of the day, tonight." Blaine nodded, eyes serious. "We'll have pizza, make a game plan, sleep."

Something inside Payne whispered, "What if these guys are ax murderers?"

"Works for me," said Will.

The other guys agreed, and they all turned to him expectantly.

Will took his hand, and he nodded. "Okay. Okay, let me grab my laptop and my chargers, huh?"

"We all going back in with him?" Will asked. "In case the door shuts and gets… let's go with 'stuck.'"

"Yeah. We stick together in the house," Jason said. "Just in case. I think we should make that the standard. Don't do anything alone, and try not to get separated."

Will nodded, and all six of them trooped back into his house.

"I'm going to stay here, holding the door open," suggested Flynn.

"Be careful, babe." Blaine kissed him. "Seriously."

Will rolled his eyes. "Honeymooners."

Flynn stuck his tongue out at Will before answering Blaine. "I'm only standing here keeping the door from closing. I'll be fine."

They all trekked to the library, where Payne grabbed his electronics, then his bedroom where he gathered up toiletries and a few clothes. It was a little ridiculous, but at the same time he was happy to not be doing this alone.

"It's like we're your bodyguards," noted Will. "Which I guess in a way we are. Though it's your spirit that seems to keep taking a hit from this thing."

"Are you going to start singing Whitney Houston?" Payne asked.

"Oh, you don't want Will to sing," Jason assured him. The other guys quickly agreed.

Payne snorted, shook his head. "I'm going to follow you guys in my car, okay? How far is it?" What was he thinking? Going to a *barn*? With virtual strangers.

"I'll drive with you," Will offered.

"Sure. Totally." He was all over that. It didn't matter that he didn't know Will all that much better than the others. Who was he kidding? No matter how much so-called real time had passed, he and Will had an entire day together under their belts.

"This way nobody has to worry about following anyone." Will handed his keys over to Darnell. "Who's picking up the pizza on the way back to Blaine's?"

"We will. If you get there first, you know where the key is."

"Thanks, Blaine." Will turned back to him. "Lead on. Gotta admit, I'm looking forward to having a drive in your ritzy vehicle.

"Ritzy? Vehicle? It's just a car." Dork.

"Well, it's a better car than I've ever ridden in. You have seen the van we go around in, right?"

"Yeah, it's… a conversation piece."

Will snorted as he settled into the passenger seat, wiggling his ass. "Wow, this has a great passenger seat. I bet if we didn't have to worry about cops and other traffic we could make it to Blaine's in record time."

"Probably. You'll have to give directions, huh?"

"Yeah, no worries. It'll take a little over an hour." Will rubbed his hands along the leather seat. "We can continue our first date."

"You still want to?" He was pleased and surprised.

"Oh. Does that mean you don't?" Will looked disappointed.

"I want to. I don't care if it was the house. I was enjoying getting to know you."

Will's expression cleared. "Oh good. I do too. And I think the fact that we still want to continue our date now that we're out of the house means it wasn't the house. If you know what I mean."

"Right. We both aren't immediately growling at each other." Just the opposite, in fact.

"Well, that was the house. I told you that you were my type." Will looked smug. "And now we have a whole hour—a whole real hour—to get to know each other better."

"Okay, we should start with the radio. What do you like to listen to?" Tunes were important, in Payne's opinion.

"I'm pretty easy, but I've always liked classical for driving."

"Oh?" He liked that. "Pick a station. I'm interested to hear your favorites."

Will fiddled with the radio until he found a station, an upbeat piece filling the car. Mozart, Payne thought. He approved.

Payne headed out onto the highway, the windows open, the wind blowing, and the world seeming… lovely. Will hummed along with the music, even made a few conducting motions with his hands. Frankly, it was adorable. Unexpected. Insane. Wonderful but insane.

Payne found himself laughing. The world seemed fresh, new. He hadn't felt this good since he'd moved into the house.

"That's still a great laugh, Professor."

"Thank you, Mr. Will. I do appreciate it."

"So what do you like to do on your downtime?" Will asked, watching him. There was something warm about that gaze, something comforting and exciting at the same time.

"Read, watch movies, bake. I'm a little bit of a homebody." If by little one understood a lot. He worked at home; he hobbied at home. Hell, there were times he made his grocery order from home and only went out to pick it up so the number of people he saw was minimal.

"You bake? I like to eat baked goods. There we go—another thing in common," Will proclaimed.

"I do. I mean, I'm learning. It's a gorgeous kitchen for baking, isn't it?" He'd made sure he'd have everything he needed for making anything, for experimenting and having fun with baking, cooking, food in general.

"I'm going to have to go with I guess so. I'm not much of a baker," Will admitted. "But it's a lovely space. Lots of room."

"It is. I put in a proving drawer and everything." Like they had on all the baking shows.

"Are you going to hate me if I tell you that I have no idea what that means?" Will asked.

"No. It's a drawer to help bread rise." He explained and drove, talking about his kitchen and the things he wanted to try, with Will listening and directing. It was lovely.

The hour went by far too quickly, and as they drove up the driveway toward a barn, he couldn't help but wish that it had been longer. A lot longer.

"This is where you live?" he asked.

"No, I've got a tiny bachelor's in town. This is Blaine and Flynn's place. Looks like a regular old barn, right? Looks totally different inside. It's kind of cool."

The van with Supernatural Explorers on the side was already there. And there were lights peeking through from inside.

"And I thought we were going to beat them here." Payne was sure that's what Will had said would happen.

"We might have taken the longer way around," Will admitted. "I hope you don't mind. I wanted to spend more time with you."

That was the nicest thing anyone had done in a long time. "I don't mind at all." He leaned over, begging a kiss.

Will leaned in too and pressed their lips together. The zing was still there, an electric shock that woke his entire body up. He gasped, opening right up for the kiss. Will cupped his cheek, fingers sliding on his skin as the kiss continued. Payne's skin tingled at every point of contact.

This wasn't the house. This had nothing to do with the house.

It was Will. Him and Will. Their chemistry together.

The kiss deepened, Will slipping his tongue between Payne's lips. Payne didn't want it to end. He reached up, cupping Will's jaw and keeping them together. Will's moan filled his mouth and made the kisses that much better. Pressing as close as he could within the confines of the vehicle, Will deepened the kiss even more, and Payne shifted to take it, which bumped his elbow into the horn.

They jumped apart at the sudden noise.

"Oh, sorry. God. Sorry. I want you." He looked into Will's eyes, then at Will's lips while he licked his own.

The other guys rushed out of the barn like a swarm of bees, coming right for them.

"Oy. I want you too, but we're going to have to put a pin in it—given we've got company." Will gave him a last quick kiss anyway.

"No fair," he complained. "We could just drive away."

Will looked mightily tempted, but then the others were at their car doors, and Will sighed. "We should eat and figure out what's going on with your ghost."

Jason banged on the car door, and Will opened it.

"Okay, okay. We're coming. God. Can't a couple of guys share a quiet moment together?"

"You beeped the horn," Jason pointed out.

Will's lips quirked up into a half smile. "Yeah, but it wasn't on purpose."

"My elbow slipped." Payne grinned, going for goofy. "Total accident."

Jason rolled his eyes but then laughed with the others. And Will touched his thigh before getting out of the car. Payne following suit.

"Are you guys feeling better now that we're away from the house?" Flynn asked.

"I am," Jason said before he or Will could say anything. "I didn't even realize I was feeling off until I wasn't anymore."

"It was a lovely drive. Seriously. We had a ball." God, how much did that suck? It was his house, and here they all were, him included, feeling better now that they were away from it.

Will's arm went around his waist like he understood. "What about you, Blaine? Have you been feeling affected at all by the stuff going on at the MacGregor house? What's your take on the whole thing?"

"I think there's definitely more than one entity. Seriously. I think we're dealing with a number of beings."

"A number? Like more than two?" Will asked, looking less than happy at that thought. "I mean, we discovered some bad stuff went on there in its early heyday, so I suppose I shouldn't be surprised. 'A number of beings' so doesn't sound like an easy fix, though."

"I think if we can deal with the malevolent ones, the others will be easier—may not even matter."

Blair held the door open for everyone, giving Payne his first glimpse of the inside of the barn. It was surprisingly comfy and cozy looking. There was even a fireplace in the living room. The furniture was mismatched and obviously lived in, but it all looked like it was made for comfort rather than style.

"This is great, guys. Seriously." It was a real homey building, somewhere to hang out.

"Not bad for a barn, eh?" Will's eyes lit up. "Pizza! We haven't eaten all day."

"It's early afternoon, Will," Darnell said dryly.

"Twenty minutes for you guys was all day for us. My stomach believes those pizzas are necessary for life."

Payne shook his head and chuckled. If he was going to get locked in his bedroom with Will again, he'd better put away a much bigger stash.

Chapter Eight

THEY chowed down on pizza and Cokes, Will finally feeling full after six slices. Crazy, but he honestly hadn't eaten all day, no matter how much time had passed for the guys. Sure he'd had snacks, but that didn't count as eating, not really. Again, it had been eight to ten hours. That was a long time without anything substantive. And who knew what the time warp did to one's body.

He wasn't going to consider how freaky the whole twenty minutes versus a whole lot of hours deal was. Ghosts were one thing, time moving differently in one room from the rest of the world was quite another. He didn't like to think about it too hard, or about that beady black eye he'd seen, though he supposed he would have to say something when they started talking shop.

On the bright side, it seemed the attraction he and Payne felt was real and not because of the house. Maybe the desperation to their first kisses had been house induced, but the chemistry seemed to be all theirs.

He and Payne were squished together in the easy chair, Payne half in his lap. Neither of them were complaining about lack of space, and Jason had stopped with the weird accusations regarding their relationship. Seemed that might have been house induced as well. Payne was dozing, heavy against him, one hand sliding and drawing shapes on his thigh.

"I don't think he's gotten much sleep." Will was feeling very protective. "Maybe we can let him get some zzz's for a bit."

"I can only imagine how exhausting all this is. Seriously." Jason shook his head, the look sympathetic.

"He's been doing it all on his own for so long. And we've all felt what it's like there." It was crazy. "I think this is the first malevolent haunting we've done. At least of this magnitude." He needed to tell them about the eye. He needed to. It was freaky and a little unbelievable, though, so he really didn't want to.

"Yeah. It's a little... unnerving really." Blaine shook his head. "Really."

"Yeah. Yeah, it affected me hard right from the start, didn't it?" He opened his mouth to keep going, to tell them about the eye. Then he closed his mouth again. God, why was this so hard? He wasn't a wuss. He wasn't a scaredy-cat. Hell, how many haunted places had he been in? Tons. He'd been able to tell Payne. Payne had believed him.

"What is it?" Jason asked.

He wasn't sure how Jason had known.

"I can read it in your face you've got something to tell us. Come on, we've known each other forever. Spill."

He cleared his throat. Three times. It felt like there was something in there, blocking his ability to speak. He growled. This was crazy. The house was over an hour's drive away. Everyone here was family, aside from Payne, who he was hoping was headed in that direction.

He laid it out there as simply as possible. No theories, no feelings, just the facts. "Okay. So while we were trapped in the bedroom…. Near the start—Payne was still unconscious and I was wandering. I tried the door, and it was locked. I couldn't get it open. Well, I looked through the keyhole, and something looked back."

Blaine stared at him. "What? Who, I mean?"

"I don't know. But it wasn't friendly. Black and beady and glaring like it was super angry. Frankly, it scared the shit out of me when I first saw it. When I looked again to be sure, it blinked. That was enough for me—I didn't look again."

Payne fussed a little in his sleep, and Will stroked his arm, soothing him.

Blaine tilted his head. "Did Payne see it?"

Will shook his head. "I told him about it, and he believed me. He didn't want to look." Not that Will blamed him. He didn't want to see it again. Ever.

"No. No, I can see that. Maybe we'll put cameras up," Darnell suggested from where he was stretched out on the floor. "That way no one gets an eye put out."

"Sounds like a plan. You guys think the big bad guy here is the original homeowner? The research showed he was a nasty man." Which was putting it mildly.

"Either that or his victims. Maybe both." Blaine chewed on his fingernail.

"Dude. That hadn't even occurred to me. You think they're after Payne because he's a direct relation?" Will blinked. "Do you know what the original owner looked like? Is it close?" They were related after all, so it would make sense if they had similar features.

Jason stared at his computer, pressing keys until his fingers suddenly stilled. "Oh my God." He turned his laptop around so they all could see. "That's Angus MacGregor, the original owner." They all leaned in to take a look. Angus MacGregor was the spitting image of Payne. Or vice versa, Will supposed.

"Dude. Dude, look at that!" Will stared at the image. He could hardly believe it. He would have thought it was actually a picture of Payne if it hadn't clearly been a digital copy of a painting. That and the style of the guy's clothing. "Dude!"

Payne snorted and woke up, shaking his head. "Wha—" He cleared his throat. "Sorry, I think I fell asleep."

Will looked at Payne, then back at the computer. "Did you know you could have been Angus MacGregor's twin?"

"Huh? I mean, I look like my dad a lot...."

"Show him, Jase."

Jason turned the laptop so Payne could see.

"I mean, he's wearing the old-time clothing, but otherwise, he could be you." Will thought it was a touch creepy how much they looked alike. Especially given what they'd read about the original MacGregor.

"Weird! That's... that could be me."

Flynn nodded. "Yeah. And if the evil presence is made up of the people who died or were hurt under Angus MacGregor's rule, they might think you're him."

"I think your grandmother is trying to help you, though. She's working hard to protect you." Blaine sighed. "I think they might have pushed her down the basement stairs, and she's trying to keep you away from them. My bet is that the basement is where the ghosts congregate. That would be where the servants would have lived."

"I really want to try and preserve the door." When they started to argue, Payne held up one hand. "Even if we have to take it off. It's an original. It's special. It's history."

"We'll go in tomorrow with equipment to take it off, then. We'll bring bolt cutters for the heavy lock and a lockpick kit, stuff to take the pins out to take the door off if we need to. Heavy duty flashlights too. We don't want anyone else taking a header down those stairs." Jason made notes as he talked.

"No. No more falling." Payne sounded very sure about that.

"Are you going to be able to handle us going down there?" Will asked Payne. "We could leave you outside the house, or even leave you here or at a restaurant somewhere."

"Why would you want to leave me behind?"

"Because every time we've gone near that basement or pushed the issue with it, you've either gone weird or passed out. We will promise to keep the door intact, but I think it's safer for you if we do this without you." Will didn't want anything hurting Payne.

Payne shook his head. "I'm not sure I can do that. My whole stomach clenches thinking about it."

"We might need him there," Blaine said softly. "If we're right, he's who the ghosts are mad at. They may not even manifest if it's just us."

Will didn't like it. He didn't like it at all. "I think that's bullshit. I think they're going to show up no matter who comes." He took Payne's hand. "I'm worried about you. You've been under the influence of that house for a long time."

"I don't know what to do," Payne admitted. "I mean, I'm totally lost."

"We've got your back, Payne. We're going to fix it for you." Will squeezed Payne's hand.

"If we can," Jason amended.

"We can and we will," Will insisted. He wasn't sure how, but Payne was... well, he was smart and he was nice and he was hot and Will liked him.

Jason gave him a warning look, but he didn't back down. He was making this promise, and he'd do everything he could to make it come true.

"Thank you. I just... it's my family estate. I'm supposed to be there."

"As long as it doesn't kill you."

"Right. No killing. At all." Payne's lips firmed. "So is this like that movie where we're going to go downstairs and find my great-great-etc. grandfather's body in the basement?"

"I think we're more likely to find the bones of the servants he worked to death," Blaine muttered. "That's my feeling."

"So what? We... bury them?" Payne asked.

"Salt and burn them first is the standard." Flynn put his plate down.

"Ew." Will and Payne spoke together.

"I know, but it needs to be done." Flynn pointed at Jason. "Make sure you add supplies for that to your list. Salt, accelerant, and matches."

"A fire extinguisher," Darnell suggested. "Just in case."

"Don't use my barbecue grill." Payne gave them all a pointed look.

Will tried not to laugh, but the others went off, and they all started laughing.

He loved how Payne was pressed against him, belly bouncing with his chuckles. He wanted to take Payne somewhere private and make love to him. And that was all him—they'd definitely left the house behind. He wanted to strip Payne down and explore him, every inch.

"So have we got our agenda set for tomorrow?" He would take Payne to a hotel. His place was tiny and Payne's was, well, crowded.

"I guess so, yeah. We can have a big slumber party here. Watch movies and all." Blaine looked so pleased.

"Oh." He glanced at Payne, seeing the bags beneath his eyes, the stress lines around his mouth. "I think I should get Payne settled at a hotel so he can get some sleep. Not that the slumber party doesn't sound like fun, but Payne looks exhausted."

Blaine blinked at him, Darnell's eyebrow lifted, but Jason just grinned.

"Payne? What do you want to do?" Will asked, letting Payne decide.

"I am pretty tired…." Oh hell yes.

Will had to keep from cheering. He couldn't control his grin, though. "I'll take you whenever you're ready."

"Yeah? Is now okay?" Payne's hand slid along his spine.

"Sure. That way we won't get sucked into Blaine's lousy taste in movies." He gave his friend a wink.

"Hey! I've got great taste!"

"In your mouth," Jason muttered.

Will chuckled as Flynn giggled, and Darnell outright cackled.

"All right guys, we're going to go. How about we meet back at the house tomorrow at eleven so we've got a lot of hours of sunlight left." That would give him and Payne a nice lazy morning tomorrow too.

"That works. We'll bring the tools." Jason gave them a little wave.

"And we'll bring ourselves." Will led Payne out, one hand on his lower back to guide him.

"That was nicely done, Will." Payne's voice was soft, amused.

"Thank you kindly." He took Payne's hand as they cleared the door. "I'm glad you're on the same page."

"I am. It's not the house."

"Yeah. I know. This is just you and me."

They got into the car. "So do we want some little no-tell motel or something medium or something ritzy?" He could go dutch for ritzy for a night.

"Let's do something nice. A big bathtub and room service. We can split it."

"We're still on the same page, Professor." He directed Payne back toward the edge of town, where there was a Hyatt.

"Good. I… I'm craving you. I want to explore, you know?"

"I hear you. It'll be good to spend time together. The two of us away from the house, away from ghosts and people. Just away."

It didn't take long to get to the hotel, and they made short work of getting a suite with a king-size bed, a huge bathroom, and twenty-four-hour room service. It was just what the doctor ordered.

They stood there in the middle of the room, looking at each other. It was like they didn't know what to do now that all the outside influences were gone.

Will finally laughed, breaking the tension. Then he pressed his lips to Payne's. It was sweet as hell, the way Payne opened up to him. He dipped his tongue into Payne's mouth, the flavor there magical.

Payne's hands pushed up into his hair, holding him close. He liked that, liked feeling precious, wanted. Moaning, he wrapped his hands around Payne's waist, fingers pressing in. He dug in harder as the kiss deepened, trying to keep his footing. Maybe they should have started this next to the bed—his knees felt weak. He liked that, liked how the simple kisses resonated through his whole body.

Opening wider, he invited Payne into his mouth. He loved Payne's flavor, the taste sweet with a hint of salt.

Payne was vocal, making happy sounds that vibrated his lips.

Will didn't know how long the kiss went on, but it was a while, like they were both reveling in it. The heat was building, but slowly, letting them enjoy the journey. Groaning, Will closed his lips around Payne's tongue and sucked on it.

Payne pulled Will's shirt out of his jeans, fingers dragging along his belly. Oh, what a tease. Will sucked in, then pushed his belly out, rolling it, giving Payne's fingers something to do, something to chase. Payne laughed, the sound happy, merry. Damn.

He let go of Payne's hips so he could pull Payne's shirt out of his slacks too. He went a little farther, though, teasing his fingers up to just below Payne's nipples.

One of those tiny nips was pierced with a single ring. "Oh, what a surprise!"

Payne blushed, the color high in his cheeks. Will kissed one cheek then the other. Careful not to touch Payne's nipple yet, he toyed with the ring. It was simple, solid, and this secretly sexy thing, and it thrilled Will to no end.

"You have any more surprises for me, Professor?"

"Do I? I hope so." Payne bit his bottom lip.

Oh fuck, that tease was so hot. Groaning, Will pounced, taking Payne's mouth again, hitting it hard enough their teeth clacked together. He pushed Payne's shirt up higher, but he couldn't take it off while they were kissing. He didn't want to give up the kissing, though, so he was stuck, his brain not able to figure things out right now.

It was okay. They had all night. All fucking night long. He walked Payne slowly backward as they kissed until his back hit the door. That let him press up against Payne as they kissed, and the door helped hold up Payne's shirt so Will could let go with one hand and get back to touching.

He tugged the ring, pulled one tiny nipple. Payne cried out, so he did it again, grinding their lower bodies together as more sounds poured into his mouth. He spread his thighs, and Payne curled one leg around him.

God, they needed to have their pants out of the way. He had a feeling that wasn't going to work out any better than their shirts had. He didn't care, though. He only cared about their dicks touching.

Grunting, he got a hand between them and tugged open buttons, pulled at their zippers. Each time his fingers fumbled against his own cock, it made him jerk.

"Oh. Get the edge off? Please?"

"God yes." Will fished into Payne's slacks, found the velvet flesh, and grabbed it. It felt so good in his hand, all that heat against his palm. Payne matched him, touch for touch, the firm fingers on his dick making him gasp.

He started jerking Payne off with long strokes, working Payne from base to tip. Every time he hit the root, he'd probe Payne's balls with his little finger. Payne widened his stance, pushing up into each touch.

So fucking hot.

Will moved faster, paying attention to every brush across his cock. Payne was leaking, aching for him, the way getting slick.

"Soon." Warning, prayer, or whatever, he let Payne know.

"Please." Payne's grip tightened, dragging along his shaft.

"Together." He grunted the word out, moving to bring their cocks together. Then he grabbed them both in his hand, squeezing hard. Payne arched, rocking up on tiptoe, driving them together.

Will bit at Payne's lips, his kiss growing desperate as he got close. He wanted to tell Payne to do it now, but he was beyond words. He grunted and shoved up against Payne as his balls emptied, come spraying up between them. Payne's orgasm joined his, heat coating his fingers.

Groaning, he rested against Payne and just breathed.

"Damn. That was… can we do it again?" Payne asked.

"God, I hope so." He laughed and rubbed their lips together quickly. "You wanna try out the bed next or the tub? If it's big enough, I hear shower sex is pretty awesome."

"Mmm. Let's get wet and slick."

"I like the sound of that." He tugged Payne's slacks back up, and closed the top button, then did the same for himself so neither of them tripped and killed themselves on the way to the shower. That would be a hell of a downer to their evening.

"Me too. I love shower sex." Payne grabbed his ass. "I like getting wet and soapy too."

"I want to get you wet and soapy." He took Payne's hand and curled their fingers together.

"What else do you want?" What a little tease.

"I want to be buried in that sweet ass of yours. I want a proper look at it first, though."

That made an impression on Payne. Excellent. He let go of Payne's hand so he could give Payne's ass a swat. It felt good, but it would feel better if Payne's ass were bare.

"Look at you!" Payne grabbed him as they got to the huge bathroom, kissed him hard.

He laughed as their lips parted. "And look at you." He grunted. "In fact, we could be looking at a lot more of each other if we got naked already."

"Picky, picky." Payne turned the water on, started it warming.

"For wanting you naked? I'll take it." Will tugged Payne's shirt off his shoulders.

He loved the visual of Payne's lean body, the pale skin, the promise of need. He kept watching as he worked on Payne's jeans next, opening that top button again and letting the front flaps fall apart. "Mmm. You are lovely."

"Not too skinny?" Payne asked.

He slid his hands around Payne's waist. His fingers didn't meet. "No, you're perfect."

Payne blushed, a smile blooming.

Leaning in, Will brought their mouths together again. He really liked kissing Payne. It made him feel good down to his toes. Fortunately, Payne seemed to be right with him, hand on his jaw, keeping them together.

While they kissed, he pushed Payne's pants down off his hips, letting gravity pull them down to Payne's ankles. Then he popped his own button and pushed at the denim, working it off.

They managed to get naked without falling or bashing each other with an elbow, and he gave them props for that even as he continued to devour Payne's mouth. They stumbled into the shower stall, the steam filling the air.

The water was almost too hot—almost—falling on them like a summer rain shower. Fuck, Payne made him positively poetic. For these kisses and the water-slick feeling of Payne's skin against his own, he'd take it.

Payne groaned, pressing tight against Will, cock making a grand recovery. Grabbing the soap, Will began slicking up Payne's skin, fingers sliding along it smoothly.

"Mmm… I love that slippery sensation."

"Me too. It's sexy as hell. You're sexy as hell." God, he'd lost his ability to not be cheesy. As long as Payne kept letting him touch, that didn't really matter.

Payne stretched up tall, letting him see, letting him touch everywhere. He leaned in to take Payne's ringed nipple into his mouth. The metal was hot from Payne's body and the water, but Payne's skin was hotter still, the hard little nipple burning against his tongue. He sucked even as he looped his tongue through the ring and tugged gently.

"Mmm…." Payne balanced, hands on Will's shoulders.

"Did you get this done to commemorate something? Or for a special someone?" He flipped the ring up and down with his tongue.

"I did it myself. I wanted to see how it looked, and I liked it."

He raised his head, staring at Payne in surprise. That was way more badass than he would have expected from Payne. "That's hot."

"Is it?"

"Fuck yes." He thought the idea of… doing that, piercing your own nipple, was amazing. "You like how it feels too, not just how it looks, eh?" He took it between his teeth again and tugged on it.

"Fuck yes!" Payne sounded shocked and so pleased.

He twisted it slightly as he tugged it again. He had a hunch he'd be playing with it a lot. It was like a button you couldn't help but press.

Payne grabbed his cock and tugged, pulling hard, making his skin burn.

"If that's supposed to discourage me from doing this—" He twisted and tugged again. "—it's not going to work."

"No?" Payne laughed. "God, I'm glad I met you."

"Ditto." Leaning in, Will licked the water from Payne's throat. He did love a hotel shower, where you didn't have to worry about running out of hot water. They could take their sweet fucking time.

Part of him whispered that it was so much easier to not be in that house, to be free. Most of him simply enjoyed the man in front of him. He wanted to do Payne up against the tile. Did they have fucking condoms? He searched his memory, trying to think if he had at least one in his wallet. Surely so. He was a healthy, reasonable man. He needed to see if the front desk had more. Though not right this second, of course.

"Don't suppose you have lube stashed in your pockets?" The hotel hand lotion would do in a pinch. "Don't suppose you're into getting fucked?"

"I am and I don't, but there's a condom in my wallet."

"We can use hand lotion or shampoo for lube." Maybe they should just rub off here and do the actual fucking in the bed, seeing as they had to go find the stuff for it.

"Uh-huh." Payne leaned out of the shower, plucked his wallet from his pocket, and retrieved the condom from his wallet.

"Oh, that was smooth." Will liked smooth on Payne. He stroked his cock. "You wanna put it on me?"

"I do." Payne opened the little package and smoothed the condom on Will with mostly confident fingers. Of course, it probably would have made more sense for him to open Payne up first, but he could work with this. He grabbed the shampoo and squeezed some on his fingers. Oh yeah, nice and slick. "Turn around. Give me your ass."

Payne turned, butt pointed out toward him. Groaning, Will pressed his fingers against Payne's hole, sliding them along the wrinkled flesh.

"I bet you're tight, babe."

"It's been a while, yeah."

"Then I'd better take some time opening you up, eh?" He rubbed that wrinkled skin some more before adding more slick to his fingers, getting ready to go in. Payne leaned, bracing himself against the sides of the tub.

Will pressed a kiss to Payne's spine, then pushed the tip of his index finger hard against the tight muscles. He kept pressing, moaning as Payne let him in. He knew it had to scrape, to burn, and he knew it had to be good.

He wriggled his fingertip inside Payne, loving the heat, the tightness of Payne gripping him. Groaning, he pushed in deeper, pulled away, pushed in again. He leaned his forehead against Payne's shoulder blade. That let him concentrate on what he was doing, the warmth of the shower put to shame by the heat of Payne's body as it pulled his finger in.

Payne took him, rocking in slow, easy, motions, soft moans joining the patter of the water. He moved with Payne, body moving back and forth.

God, they were so much hotter than the water.

He pushed a second finger in with the first. He was trying to take his time, but he wanted inside so badly. He'd make sure to open Payne up properly, though. No hurting. Only pleasure.

He played his fingers inside Payne, pushing and stretching them apart. Payne was so tight and so hot. Payne went up on tiptoe, rocking up, reaching for the showerhead. It gave Will a gorgeous view of long, lean lines. Will used his free hand to stroke Payne from shoulder to ass, then to rub Payne's belly and tickle up his sides.

Payne's ass clenched around him as he laughed. "Will!"

He chuckled and pushed his fingers deeper into Payne, looking for the man's gland to contrast with the tickling. Payne twisted, crying out, the sound a little desperate.

Aha! There. That was exactly what he was looking for. He stayed at that spot, pinging it repeatedly.

"Will! Will, come on! Your cock. Give me your fucking cock." Demanding, filthy words. He loved it.

"Gotta make sure you're ready. Won't hurt you."

"Please, babe. Please. I'm ready."

"Mmm. Okay, okay. Keep your pants on... or off as it happens." He giggled at himself—actually giggled—as he tugged his fingers away.

"Butthead." Payne laughed with him, though, didn't he?

He added more of the shampoo to his cock, then put the head against Payne's hole, pressing, but not enough to actually push in yet. Payne bore back and took him in, the head of his cock popping through. He moaned as that tight heat gripped him. What had been good around his fingers was even better around his cock.

He grabbed on to Payne's hips, driving them together, harder and faster. His balls swung as he thrust, his need soaring. Payne managed to get one hand around himself. Will could see his arm moving in time with the thrusts. He wanted to see that. Next time. Next time he'd watch.

He rested his forehead on Payne's back and slammed in with everything he had.

"Soon. Fuck, man. Soon." He could feel Payne's body milking him.

"Yeah, that's good. I'm ready. You're amazing." The words poured out of him, one after the other.

Payne's ass clenched around him like a fist, squeezing him tight.

"Oh fuck! Gonna!" It was all he got out before he slammed in hard, filling the condom.

They swayed together, both of them moaning softly as the water sluiced down around them.

He didn't want to come out, but the way they were standing it was going to happen whether he wanted it to or not. So, he grabbed the base of his cock and pulled out with a groan.

"God, that's the weirdest sensation...."

"Me coming out?" Will had to admit he'd never been on the receiving end. Probably because he looked like a biker and guys assumed he didn't bottom.

"Uh-huh. I love to be full."

"Well, I loved filling you." He put a kiss on Payne's spine. "All good things, eh?"

"Yes. All good things." Payne's voice lowered. "I'm glad it wasn't just the house."

"God, me too." He squeezed Payne in a tight hug, then stepped back and stripped off the condom. They both rinsed off quickly, and then Will turned the water off. "Let's see what the towels are like."

"As much as this place cost us, they'd better be cushy!"

He grabbed one. Oh yeah, cushy. Pleased, he wrapped it around Payne before grabbing one for himself. They dried each other off, leaning a bit, playing some. It was fun and easy and more than a little wonderful.

They eventually made it to the bed, and they lay there, snuggled under the covers, nuzzling, kissing, touching.

"Thank you for suggesting this. I appreciate it." Payne wrapped around him, holding on.

"I thought we deserved some time to figure out whether we had something together or if it was all the house."

"It's not an evil place. My gram… she was a fab lady."

"I'm sure she was. You know about the history of the house, though, right?" Payne had to—he was a researcher after all. And they'd talked about it a lot. Still, sometimes it felt like Payne had forgotten there was reason for angry ghosts. "There was a lot of bad there. Probably in the basement. I still think your gram has been protecting you. That's what Blaine thinks, and he's good with ghosts." That was why they were going to check the downstairs out. "But that's tomorrow. Tonight is just you and me."

"Tomorrow you'll be with me, right?"

"Every step of the way. And if I turn into Mr. Asshole again, ignore me, okay? You know that's not me."

"Fair enough." Payne hugged him. "I'm scared of that basement. I always have been."

"I think there's a good reason for that. We'll make it yours again, Payne." He held on to Payne, stroking the long line of his spine.

Payne was quiet after that, and Will continued to hold him, to touch him. He wanted to ground himself in this—in what was real between the two of them—in preparation for being in the house again tomorrow morning. In preparation for confronting the ghost—or ghosts—on what was probably their home turf.

But that was tomorrow. He wasn't going to worry about it until then.

Chapter Nine

THE temptation to beg Will to stay in the hotel had been huge. Huge. He couldn't afford it—not money-wise and not emotionally. This was his home they were going back to, and he couldn't afford to be afraid of it.

Still. The time they'd spent together in the hotel had been... not magical, because that could be taken too literally, but it had been wonderful. Just two guys with crazy chemistry getting to know each other better, both in and out of bed.

And he liked Will. A whole hell of a lot. What if Will the jerk came back when they went into the house? He knew Will had told him to ignore that kind of behavior, but that was easier said than done.

What happened if he went in and just passed out? What if he passed out and never woke up again?

"Payne!"

Fingers snapped in front of Payne's face, making him gasp and jerk.

"You were a million miles away, Professor. We're here. We've been here for the last few minutes, but it's like I've been talking to myself." Will looked into his eyes. "Are you with me?"

Payne glanced out the car window at his house. It was beautiful in the morning light, but that beauty hid something horrible. "I'm scared. Stupid, huh?" He tried to grin.

"I don't think it's stupid to be scared of ghosts. Especially when there's some nasties in the mix. I'm not going to let anything happen to you, though. I swear it."

"Okay. I believe you." He wanted to believe, anyway.

"Good. The guys just pulled up. Let's go kick some ghostly ass."

Payne nodded and ducked his head. He could handle this. He was a stud. He'd done just fine on his own for months before he'd had help. Now he had five guys with him. He could do this.

They got out of the car and met up with the rest of the guys, who were unloading supplies from the van. Along with the cameras and ghost-hunting equipment was what looked like a hardware store's worth of bolt cutters and flashlights, shovels, and even a bat.

"This is just in case." Will fondled the bat.

"You're molesting the wood," Darnell teased. "You're a lucky man, MacGregor."

Payne blushed at Darnell's words, and Will rolled his eyes.

"You're just jealous, D."

"Of a bat that's gotten more action in the last thirty seconds than I've had in the last three months? You better believe I'm jealous." Darnell leered comically at the bat.

Everyone laughed, and it helped ease some of the tension that had been building.

"How are you doing, Payne?" Blaine asked. "Are you holding up okay?"

"Yeah. Last night was a good sanity break."

Will gave him a warm smile. So maybe it had been more than a sanity break. It had been exactly what Payne had needed, and he wouldn't change a thing. Aside from having stayed there, of course.

"Okay. You need to breathe and try to stay with us." Blaine gave him a warm smile.

Will nodded. "Give me your hand, and if you start feeling weird at all, squeeze."

"You aren't going to film?" Jason asked.

"I've got it." Darnell grabbed the better of the two cameras. "I think we need as many hands on deck to keep weird stuff from happening as possible. More than we need two cameras, anyway."

Jason considered that for a moment, then nodded. "Yeah, I guess that works. It'll give it an air of cinema verité if we only have footage from the one camera too."

"Thank you. I… It's good to know Will is right here."

"I've got you," Will growled.

He reached out and took Will's hand, holding on. Will nodded, hefting the bat in his other hand. He put it over his shoulder and squeezed Payne's hand.

They headed in. The house seemed insanely quiet and still, their footsteps loud.

"You feel anything, Blaine?" Jason asked in a hushed tone.

"I feel… like something's waiting."

"Great," muttered Will. Then he straightened and gave Payne a fierce smile. "Bring it on."

"Right? This is my house. Mine." Dammit. He was going to let the ghosts know that in no uncertain terms.

"Let's go let the ghosts know." Jason nodded and led the way, Blaine falling into step next to him.

They got through the door and moved toward the hall where the basement door was. They'd only just started down the hall when the front door slammed closed, making Payne jump.

"Oh God." He hated this. He hated being scared all the time.

"Easy, Professor. We're all right here, and nothing is going to hurt you." Will swung his bat once.

The chandelier above them swung without provocation, and Payne gripped Will's hand tighter, hurrying him into the kitchen.

"Okay. We need to go to the basement and cut open the lock now," Jason said. "We stay together."

You can't go to the basement.

"Leave me alone. We're going to go down there." See him take charge against the things in his house that went bump in the night.

They all turned to look at him.

"What?"

"Who are you talking to?" Will asked.

"I…. You didn't hear it?"

"Just you, Professor. And it sounded like you were replying to someone. Only none of us said anything." Will spoke quietly, gently.

"Oh." God, he was embarrassed.

"What did you hear?" Jason asked, and Darnell focused the lens on him.

"I thought...." Maybe he was imagining things. Maybe he hadn't really heard it and his mind was playing tricks on him.

"We all believe in ghosts here, hmm? You can tell us what you heard." Will squeezed his hand again.

"Someone told me not to go to the basement."

"Did they sound angry or worried?" Will asked.

"Just sure that I shouldn't go down there."

Will looked at the others, and Blaine shrugged. "Could be his grandmother looking out for him or the malevolent ghosts trying to keep him from finding their lair."

"Either way, I'm opening that door." He had to gird his loins, right? He wasn't going to freak. He wasn't going to panic.

"That's the spirit," Will said. "No pun intended."

They both chuckled, but it felt forced, not like their happy laughter of the night before. He held on to that memory.

Everyone trooped to the basement door and stopped in front of it. Will squeezed his hand, holding on almost painfully tight. "Stay with me, okay, Professor?"

"I swear to try."

"Do you want the honors?" Jason asked, offering over the bolt cutters.

Payne reached for the tools, his hands shaking violently.

Will's hand landed on his back, warm and solid and very much there. "Darnell or I could do this part if you want. We've a bit more muscle."

He shook his head. He wanted to do this. He was pretty sure he needed to do this. He had to meet this head-on and face it down. Right?

"Stay with me," he begged, a part of him feeling like a big baby for needing that, the rest of him on board with not having to deal with any ghosts on his own.

If you bring them downstairs, I'll kill them all.

"We are right here and not going anywhere," Will promised, hand remaining on his back. "You can do this."

It was hard to ignore that voice, which wasn't quite in his head—it was coming from outside of him, even if no one else could hear it. Could the ghost actually kill people?

Got your gram, didn't I?

"I've changed my mind. I don't want you guys here." A dull panic filled him, and he backed away. "I'll do it, but you guys have to leave."

"What? No. No, I'm not leaving you to do this alone." Will rubbed his back some more, hand warming a line along his spine. "Safety in numbers, Professor, remember? Besides, the five of us have done this kind of thing before. We're ready for anything. Go ahead and break the lock."

"Will's right. We're here for you." Darnell kept filming but everyone else hefted their flashlights and shovels and bats.

"The ghost will hurt you. I like you." God, his heart hurt.

"Is it threatening you?" Will asked. "I'll kill it."

"It's already dead," Jason pointed out dryly.

"Well, then, I'll send it to hell where it belongs. Is that better?" Will asked. He was growling and sounded much like had the other night when they'd first met. "Unless everyone here is too much of a chickenshit to meet this head-on. It's no fucking skin off my nose if we pack up and leave the scaredy-cat here to deal with his own problems." Will sounded more belligerent with each passing second.

"Will!" Jason grabbed Will and pulled him aside. "This isn't you."

Flynn signed and gave Payne an apologetic look. "You know that's not him, right? The ghost is trying to use him against you."

Blaine nodded. "It's scared. We're going down into the basement and it's worried we're going to find what we need to banish it."

"Take Will out," Payne demanded. "Just take him out and we'll go." He was probably going to die down there anyway, and that would be easier to take knowing Will was safe.

"You don't want me there, MacGregor, you asshole? I don't need to be there." Will threw the bat he was holding down the hall, where it hit the wall hard, and stomped off, grumbling under his breath the entire way. They all heard the front door slam.

"I don't know why it chose Will, but clearly that thing thought it could use him to keep us away from you." Jason sighed. "We can't lose anyone else, though. There is strength in numbers. Are you okay to keep going?"

"Yeah. Just keep him away from here." He hadn't liked anyone so much in a lifetime. He wasn't going to risk Will.

"This asshole version of him isn't real. You know that, right?" Jason looked concerned. "He doesn't mean the things he said."

It hit him that Jason thought he didn't want Will around because he was being a jerk again. Ironic really, because the truth was about as far away from that as could be.

"It doesn't matter. Let's do this thing." He grabbed the lock and pressed the jaws of the bolt cutters together as hard as he could, the edges of the metal digging in. It was a lot more difficult than he'd thought it would be. Than he thought it should be, in fact.

Jason set down his flashlight and shovel and put his hands beneath Payne's, adding his strength to the cutters. The metal seemed to fight them, almost creaking, and for a moment Payne thought it wasn't going to work even with both of them trying to cut through the lock. Then all of a sudden the metal gave, and the blades slid through the rest of the lock like butter.

The sudden success had Jason off-balance, and he jerked into Payne, the two of them hitting the door together. It creaked for a moment, and Payne thought it was going to open and send him headfirst down the stairs. But Darnell's hand wrapped around his arm and tugged him back, and Flynn and Blaine caught Jason, righting him.

"Christ," muttered Jason.

"This sucks, guys. I'm so sorry…." He hadn't meant for anyone to get hurt.

"You don't have to apologize," Blaine told him. "We all know you're not responsible for any of this. And if we didn't need to get down there to figure out who this ghost is and how to get rid of it, I'd suggest boarding the door up and never going down there again. But I think we all know that's not going to work. This thing is obviously affecting people and things up here. So we need to go down."

"We sure do. I'm not letting Payne continue to live under the thumb of this fucking ghost." Will came down the hall and went past them, grabbing his bat.

"Should you be here, Will?" Jason asked.

"I felt more myself when I got outside, so I chugged the holy water we had in the van. Just let this thing try to get in my head again."

"Go away!" Payne said. "I don't want you in here." He took Will's arm, shook him. "You could be hurt."

"And so could you. I would never forgive myself if I didn't go down with you and something happened to you." Will grabbed his arms and kissed him, then stared into his eyes as he continued. "We will go down there, all of us together, and take out this motherfucker. His time to be on this earth is over. Let's do this."

"This isn't the house," Payne whispered, holding Will's gaze.

Will didn't look away, not even for a second. "No, this is me and you. The growling at you earlier, that was the house. This is me now. I am clear on that." Will smiled at him. "Let's do this. You and me together."

He nodded, still holding Will's hand, and pulled the dangling chain the lock had been keeping in place off the door. It slid down with a rattle and a series of dull thuds. He took a breath to fortify himself and opened the creaky old door. The stench of dank rot belched up, nearly sending him to his knees.

Will kept holding his hand, and that stopped him from falling.

"You want one of us to go first?" Jason asked.

"We've got this," Will said. "Give me one of those monster flashlights." He put down the bat and grabbed the flashlight Jason handed him.

Payne looked down the old stairs leading into the dark basement like a maw into a devouring mouth. "So many secrets," he muttered.

"Yeah. The research we did was all too general to point to anything certain. There's a bunch of candidates for the evil ghost." Will turned on the flashlight and shone it down the stairs. "You ready for what we might find down there?"

"Uh-huh." Payne took a step forward. Immediately what felt like a dozen hands grabbed him and tried to drag him down the stairs.

His feet went out from under him, but Will dropped the flashlight and grabbed him around the waist with both hands, holding him close until he could get his feet back under him.

The flashlight bounced all the way down, leaving a swath of light across the basement floor.

"They were pulling at me," he whispered. "Someone. Lots of someones."

"Christ." Will held on to him even tighter. "Did you guys hear that?"

"Yeah." Jason turned on his flashlight and shone it down the stairs, adding to the light. "We knew that a lot of servants died down there because of the awful conditions and then the fire. There might actually be a lot of ghosts, given what you felt."

"Acting as one entity," murmured Blaine. "That's why we thought it was just one bad ghost. They're all tangled together. They're mad at Angus MacGregor. They blame him. You look so much like him…. Even now I think your grandmother is trying to keep you from going down there. I think she's the one who threatened Will to keep you from going down." Blaine swayed slightly, Flynn bolstering him on one side.

They'll kill you. Stay away. Stay out of the basement. Danger, little boy. Danger.

Payne saw himself as a little boy, staring down into the basement, the glow of the furnace like hellfire, and his gram turning him away.

"She's trying to keep me from being hurt." He blurted the words out, Will's arms never losing their grip on him.

"Yes." Blaine sounded far away. "She'll do almost anything to keep you from going down there. I don't blame her. The malevolence coming from the basement is palpable. Something's holding them to this plane. We need to go down to find out what. Make them go away."

"Does he need to come with us?" Will asked. "I could take him back out, let him sit in the car until we've dealt with it."

"I don't know, Will. I honestly don't." Now Blaine sounded sad.

"I'm not letting you go down there alone," Payne insisted. He wasn't going to lose Will. The fear that he might was real. And stronger than his fear of what they would find down there.

"I won't be alone. I've got the guys."

Payne shook his head vehemently. "No. If you go, I go."

"Well, then, I guess we go. Because it's pretty damn clear there is something down there, something bad, and we need to deal with it."

"Okay, then. Let's do this." Jason pushed past Payne and Will. "I'll go first, then Blaine and Flynn, then the two of you. Darnell will bring up the rear with the camera."

"Please God, keep us all safe." Payne wasn't a religious man, but… it seemed necessary.

"Amen," grumbled Will.

Jason led the way, Blaine and Flynn behind him, all three of them lighting up the stairs. Then Will moved the two of them forward together, one arm wrapped around Payne's waist.

Every step downward, he could feel something trying to pull him back up in the other direction. Then the screaming began, but clearly it was only in his head because no one else seemed to notice.

No. No. No. Come back upstairs. Don't go down there. Bad. Bad. No.

His knees buckled, and he reached up, clinging to Will. "Please. Please help me."

Will supported him and stopped. "Blaine?"

"We're almost at the bottom, I think he needs to come with us," Blaine called back up to them.

"Dammit." Will kept going down, practically carrying him.

The world was bashing at him, beating at his brain, and he closed his eyes. He didn't understand any of this. Not a bit of it.

"Stay with me, Professor. We're here. We're at the bottom of the stairs. No more falling down." Will squeezed him tight.

Maybe the worst was over. *Please let the worst be over.*

The guys shone the flashlights all around, and Blaine took a few steps forward. He gasped suddenly, nearly collapsing. Flynn's quick move to support him seemed to be the only thing keeping him up.

"It's bad," Blaine managed to get out. "So much pain. So many lost souls."

All your fault.

No. No, he'd just moved in a while ago.

All your fault.

"What's wrong?" Will asked. "You're shaking."

"They're saying it's his fault," murmured Blaine. "They want him dead."

Will gasped, then shouted, "No fucking way. He's not Angus MacGregor, you assholes!"

Things suddenly began to fly at them—aluminum dishes and a few pieces of wood, rocks. Will shielded Payne from the worst of it and began dragging him back toward the stairs. "I'm taking him back upstairs before they succeed in killing him."

ALL YOUR FAULT!

The sound was huge, knocking Payne's brain around in his head, and the world went blessedly black.

Chapter Ten

"I'M getting him out of here." Will grabbed Payne up and threw him over one shoulder in a fireman's carry. It was the safest way he could think of to get Payne back up the stairs.

"We're going to investigate some more. See if we can figure this out before it's too much for Blaine."

Will didn't care—he needed to get Payne out of this toxic environment. If they were lucky, things would calm down once Payne was out of the house, and the guys would be able to figure out how to stop this.

He tripped twice going up the stairs but managed to fall forward and catch himself both times. He didn't believe for a minute that was him losing his footing so much as whatever was down there trying to keep Payne with them.

The urge to slam the door shut behind him when he got to the top of the stairs was huge, but he didn't. Instead, he propped it open with a chair. He didn't trust that something wouldn't try and close the door again once Payne was safely upstairs, sacrificing the guys in order to save Payne.

He patted Payne's shoulder, his cheek. "Wake up. Come on, Professor. Wake up." He shook his head when that didn't have any effect and took Payne outside, breathing a sigh of relief when the front door opened without any problem. "Come on."

He dragged the little hall table over to prop the door open, then went onto the porch. He put Payne down on one of the huge old-fashioned porch chairs and patted his cheek again, then a little harder. "Come on. Come on. Don't you let this house get the better of you."

Payne groaned softly. "We have to go back in."

"I think you're safer if you stay out here. I'll go back and help the others." He didn't want to put Payne at any more risk.

"No. No, they want me. They're going to hurt your friends."

"They can't have you. Their beef is with your great-whatever grandfather. You're not him. And you shouldn't have to pay for the shit he did."

"No, but you and your team shouldn't either." Payne stood, swaying as soon as he was upright, nose bleeding in a single line.

Will wiped the blood away with his sleeve. "They've got each other, and they're only going to stay as long as they can safely." He was pretty sure they wouldn't be getting rid of the ghosts today, but if they could pick up enough information, hopefully they could get what they needed to come back and take care of it once and for all.

A wild cry sounded, and they both blinked.

Payne shook his head. "Come on, Will. We can't let them get hurt."

Will nodded. He didn't want Payne to go back in there, but the guys needed him. Needed both of them. "Okay. Yeah. Let's go."

Payne took his hand. "I swear to God, Will, this is ridiculous."

"No, it's not. Bad things happened in that basement, and when they died, those people didn't cross over properly. They're hurting and confused, and all the men in your family look exactly alike. From what I understand, ghosts don't experience time the way we do. They won't understand that you're not him." Will hoped talking about it would distract Payne as they approached the basement again.

"No, I'm not him. I'm a librarian. I'm a good guy."

"I know that. They don't." Maybe that's why he'd been so angry and growly when he'd first met Payne. Maybe these unfortunate ghosts had been inside him. God, that was not something he had ever wanted to be involved in.

They got back to the door to the basement. "Ready for take two?"

"Yes. Let's do this." Payne frowned mightily. "Back the fuck off, you assholes!" This fierce side of Payne was unexpected but definitely hot.

Hoping that would buoy them both, Will didn't stop at the door to the basement but went straight down. It was much easier to get down than it had been to go up.

They found Jason lying on the floor, head bleeding. Darnell was swinging the camera back and forth among Jason, the stairs, and deeper into the basement.

"Oh my God! What happened?" Will asked.

"I don't know. He just dropped. And I don't know where Blaine and Flynn went."

"They're missing? Blaine! Flynn!" Will called out for the guys. He grabbed Jason's flashlight and began throwing light around the room, searching for them. "Blaine! Call out. Flynn! Dude. Come on."

God, this place was vast, a bunch of dark little rooms. He was going to have to go searching.

"Are you going to be okay here with him?" he asked Darnell.

"I'm fine. Scared, but fine."

Will went over to his friend and hugged him, taking himself as much comfort as he hoped he was giving. "He's still breathing. He's okay."

He looked at Payne, who was crouched next to Jason. "You coming with me?" He was torn between insisting that Payne do so and wanting him to stay here and go no deeper into the basement. He also probably should have grabbed the camera, but he thought it was more important to have the flashlight and a free hand. Just in case.

"Yes. We have to figure this out."

"Okay, then. You walk behind me, but keep your hand on my shoulder so I know you're still with me."

"We'll find Blaine and Flynn first, right?"

"Absolutely. I'm sure they're just around the corner." He waited until Payne's hand gripped his shoulder, then he headed to the rooms on the left. He was going to sweep the rooms systematically.

They were tiny, dark, and his flashlight revealed walls covered with drawings and jumbled-up letters. There were no windows, no source of light, only a heavy gloom. It broke his heart to see the proof that children had lived down here as well as adults.

Everything was covered in dust, but in several rooms there was a layer of soot as well, proof of the rumored fire. God, he couldn't imagine living down here, let alone what it must have been like when the fire started. If the fire didn't get you, the smoke would have, and they'd had nowhere to go.

This was MacGregor's fault. The thought hit him like a wave. MacGregor's fault. He nodded and growled. "This should never have happened."

"I know. I don't know how anyone could be so mean." Payne's voice was little more than a whisper.

"MacGregor did it. He needs to be punished." A wave of anger rolled through him, pushing everything else away.

It wasn't merely a feeling anymore either; he could sense the chant in his bones, and then he could hear it. Dozens of voices, repeating the same thing over and over.

Kill him. Kill him. Kill him.

The rage built inside him, growing every time the chant was repeated. He whipped around. MacGregor was right there. He grabbed the flashlight tight in his hand—it would be the perfect weapon.

"Will?" Payne asked. "What is it?"

Payne.

Kill him.

MacGregor had to die. Will held the flashlight tighter.

Kill him. Kill him.

"What's wrong, babe?" Payne stepped closer.

Will's head was about to explode, the anger a living thing inside him. He raised the flashlight, ready to swing it, to bean MacGregor over the head and be done with the evil man.

No! No, this was Payne. His Payne. Will wasn't a killer, and he certainly wasn't going to kill Payne. He growled, and the rage flew off him as if a dozen hands had ripped away from him. They made for Payne.

Will shook his head. Oh no, he didn't think so.

"Run!" he shouted it as loud as he could, swinging the flashlight in front of him. He swore he could see it move through a half-dozen different forms at least, and they were all going for Payne. "Get out!"

Payne's eyes went wide at the sight. He turned tail and ran even as the hands reached him, grabbing at him. As if the ghosts had decided to divide their efforts, some of them assaulted Will again. He roared, the effort of keeping the ghosts and their anger out of him actually dropping him to his knees.

Kill him. Kill him. Kill him. The voices continued, and Will shook with it, with the fury that was building once again inside him. He wouldn't fucking let them have him, though. He knew Payne wasn't Angus, and he wasn't going to let these assholes have Payne, let alone use *him* to get it done.

He knelt there, trying to breathe, trying to see past the mist of rage in front of his eyes, his entire body shaking. The voices got louder, the anger all-consuming. It felt like his head was going to explode, the pain echoing the emotions roiling inside him and around him.

The agony grew, and he couldn't see past it, couldn't hear anything beyond the ringing sound of the mob. Still, he wouldn't let them move him. He was not their puppet or their ride or in any way their route to Payne. Louder, higher, everything built until all of a sudden it stopped and he slid into oblivion.

Chapter Eleven

PAYNE ran toward the stairs, stumbling along. He felt the air move as the ghosts reached for him, the hair on the back of his head moving, things grabbing at his ankles, his legs, trying to trip him up. He knew if he stopped moving, they'd get him.

Okay.

Okay.

Gram was right. He was going to die down here in the basement.

Kill him!

Payne could hear them, the words echoed in a dozen voices, more. They all wanted him dead. It made him want to scream and cry, but he didn't have that luxury.

Darnell and Jason were at the base of the stairs, shovels in hand, swinging at the air. He swore he could see sparkles as ghosts dissipated when the shovels went through them, then coalesced back together again.

Fuck, the stairs were lousy with them. He ducked into the shadows and headed toward the back. He heard footsteps coming in his direction. Mumbles. Were they real? Was it possible for ghosts to have footsteps? He didn't know what to do.

"Please. I'm not him. I'm not a bad guy."

A hard hand grabbed him as he slid deeper into the basement. Not the ghosts. It was Blaine who had wrapped his fingers around Payne's arm. "Gotta get out," Blaine whispered.

Kill him. Kill him. Kill him.

"You've got to get out," Blaine said again, eyes anguished. "They'll kill you."

Something pulled Blaine away from him and sent him stumbling backward. Luckily Flynn was right there to catch him, but they both went down, and the refrain got louder.

Kill him. Kill him.

Payne slipped into a tiny room and slammed the door shut behind him. He pressed his back against it, keeping it closed. "Please, God. Please let me get out of this."

I told you not to come down here. I told you it was dangerous.

He could almost see his grandmother in front of him, the air seeming to shimmer. There was definitely a tiny bit of light there—the only light in the room.

"I know. What do I do? I have to fix this." Aside from the danger to himself, he couldn't leave all these ghosts here like this. It was awful.

Always researching. Always looking for things.

Now wasn't exactly the time to be doing research when he had God knew how many angry ghosts trying to kill him "Not helpful, Gram."

Always looking for answers.

"Goddammit."

All of a sudden there was banging on the door, and he squeezed his eyes shut. *Come on. Come on. She's trying to help.*

"What answers, Gram? What am I trying to find?"

The history of a place is important. You always say.

The shimmering moved to the back of the room, then disappeared altogether. Now even his gram had abandoned him. Bur she reappeared in the same area, again just the glimmer of air where it should have been pitch black.

Okay. Okay. Back there. Was she trying to show him something? He felt around and found a barrel, which he rolled toward the door to block it, trapping himself inside and the ghosts out there. Payne wasn't sure it would keep them out indefinitely, but maybe it would take them a little while to gather their energies at least. He wished he knew more about how ghosts worked, but for now he'd have to trust Gram's knowledge. After all, she was a ghost too.

Payne didn't know what he was going to do next, but for now, this wasn't the worst thing. He hoped the guys were able to get safely upstairs, that the ghosts were concentrating on trying to get to him.

Look, child. Research. Discover.

Okay. Obviously there was more. He was loath to shuffle away from the relative safety of the barrel, but he did. He went back to the corner where she had disappeared and reappeared.

He looked around, but he couldn't see anything. It was too dark, and what little light his gram's ghost had provided had disappeared with her. He searched instead with his hands, trying to find something, anything.

In the hard packed dirt, he found the corner of something hard, something buried, and he started digging with his fingertips, trying to unearth it. He got enough of it uncovered to discover it was a covering of some sort, and when he got his finger beneath it, he could feel cool air against them.

There was another way out.

Fuck yes.

He pulled the cover away. From the greasy texture, he decided it was a piece of oilcloth, so old it crackled and shattered at his touch, the back of it fuzzy with mold and crawling with insects. Beetles, he imagined, as many tiny legs skittered across his hand. Oh God.

Oh God, he couldn't go down there…. The door across the room from him began to groan, the barrel sliding audibly across the floor.

Okay, maybe he could go down there after all.

He took his sweater off and wrapped it around his head so the bugs couldn't get into his hair. Then he wrapped the arms around his mouth and nose and tied it in the back of his head. Hopefully that would hold it in place.

Then he eased himself down carefully. It wasn't a long drop, thankfully, and as he'd hoped, he found himself in a dirt tunnel beneath the basement floor, tall enough to stand in, but barely. He wondered briefly who had dug this tunnel and for what purpose. But the curious researcher in him was overwhelmed by his need to escape at the moment. Answers would have to wait.

Spiderwebs filled the tight burrow, but Payne refused to panic. He pushed forward into the darkness. There was air. That meant there had to be a way out.

He made slow progress, tripping over things. Since he couldn't see them, he had no idea what they were. He decided they were clumps of dirt. That was safest.

The tunnel appeared to be gradually slanting upward. The breeze got stronger, and he could see a little bit of light up ahead. He hurried toward it, things snapping beneath his feet. Either the dirt ceiling above him was lowering or the floor below was rising to meet it because he soon had to crouch down to keep moving. Then his progress was halted by a grate made of thick steel. The bushes above the grating let in enough light for him to see that he was indeed trapped.

It also showed him what he'd been tripping over. Bones. Human bones.

"Oh God. Oh God. Okay. Oh God." He grabbed the grate and started shaking it hard, praying for rusted bolts, crumbled soil, something. "I'll get you all out of here. If you help me with the grate, I'll get you out of this basement. I promise."

No wonder there were ghosts here. He'd assumed most of them had died in the fire, and some must have, surely, but the rest of them were here, only steps away from a freedom they could never reach. How long had they been here before they'd finally died?

"I'm not him. I'm not him. Please help me get us out of here." He wrapped his hands around the grating and put all his weight into it. Pushing up, then pulling down, using his bent legs for leverage. It could have been his imagination, but he thought he felt it give, just a little.

And he swore he could hear them coming for him behind him in the tunnel.

"Please. My name is Payne. I'm going to get you out of here. I'm Annette's grandson." He rattled harder at the bars. They was definitely some movement, but he couldn't imagine it was going to be enough. Not to get him through. And then there were the bushes to get through too. They had to be incredibly thick, given he'd never even known this tunnel was here.

So many bones. They shouldn't be here.

He knew that. He understood that the servants had been trapped in here. Had probably starved to death. It had no doubt been awful.

"It's terrible. I'll get you out. Tell your stories. There's got to be records. I'll make it right. We have to get this damn thing loose first." He yanked hard and while it might have shifted a fraction, he didn't think he was strong enough to pull it right out like he needed to. He also thought he was running out of time. It felt like the ghosts were getting closer, screaming after him.

Maybe he could use one of the bones as a lever? It was a gruesome thought, but he was running out of time, and he was definitely out of ideas.

Get them out. Get the bones out. Out. Out. Out.

He supposed it was as good an idea as he was going to get. "Okay, Gram. I'll do it."

He grabbed handfuls of... ugh... former people and started shoving them out of the tunnel as best he could, pushing them between the bars of the grating and as far as the bushes would let him. Legs and arms and jaws and....

"The skulls won't fit!"

Out. Out. Out.

She was no help. He already knew he had to get them out. He really didn't want to have to break the bones to get them through the grating.

"Goddamnit! Motherfucker!" He grabbed one of the bars of the grate and pulled as hard as he could, and it popped free. That was enough. That was enough to wedge the skulls through.

Somehow he did it, tossed them all out into the bushes, praying that was what was needed to get the ghosts to give him a break. He tripped over another bone when he took a step back, so he went to his hands and knees, feeling around the disgusting floor of the tunnel, searching as best he could. He came across one more skull—such a small head, it had to belong to a child—and several more undetermined bones, all of which he pushed through the grating, getting them out.

Freeing them.

He hoped to God that's what he was doing anyway.

If doing this let them take over the world or become zombies or something, he was burning the house down and moving to the Bahamas.

He stayed where he was, breathing in the fresh air that came through the grating, and waited. He had no clue how he'd know if the ghosts had let the guys go once he'd thrown their bones out of the tunnel. What if he was stuck in here and died just like they had? Maybe he'd become the new ghost that haunted this place.

At that point, he was scared and tired, and he wanted a bath and to go to bed for a week. Only he wasn't sure he'd be able to sleep in this house. And that was a depressing thought.

He went to work on pulling out another bar. His hands were destroyed, he was filthy, and he had bugs everywhere. He had to admit, though, it didn't feel like there was an army breathing down his neck, coming for him. Nothing was grabbing at him, and the chaotic call to kill him had faded away.

"Payne? Where are you?"

"Professor? Please tell me you're alive."

"Call out, Payne!"

It was the guys. They were okay. The ghosts hadn't eaten them. Or had they? How did he know it was really the Supernatural Explorers?

"Professor! Oh fuck, please tell me you're alive." Will sounded honestly worried.

"Payne?" The call came to him along the tunnel. They'd found his bolt hole.

He grabbed the bar that he'd worked out. He wanted to be prepared for anything. For if it wasn't Will and the others. What if the ghosts had gotten them and they were ghosts now too. "Yeah. Go on out. I'll come up."

"Oh thank God we found you. I thought they'd gotten you. There were so many of them." He could see Will now, a dark hulking shadow.

"Still alive. If you guys will go upstairs and out, you'll see that I've thrown a bunch of bones into the bushes that we need to deal with."

Will wasn't listening, climbing right toward him, and he brandished his pipe.

"Hey, hey, Professor, it's okay. It's me. I swear."

"Yeah. Cool." He tried to let go of the pipe, but his fingers wouldn't open. "I really want to get out of here, man."

"Of course." Will wrapped a hand around his arm and tugged him in for a hug. He stiffened, trying to remember how to breathe. All he had to do was get out of here. Get upstairs. Get them outside and out of here.

Will grabbed his hand and slowly uncurled his fingers from the pipe, then he did the same thing with the other. Finally, Will led him out of the tunnel toward light and voices. The way back seemed so much shorter than it had when he'd made his way through in the first place.

He didn't speak to anyone until he was up the stairs and in the library. Then he pulled the sweater off his head and threw it right in the trash can. "The bones are outside. All of them." He hoped. He felt shell-shocked. So many of them, and they'd wanted him dead.

"We should salt and burn the bones, and bury them," Jason suggested, looking grim.

"Whatever we need to do. Come on." He grabbed a bucket from next to the fireplace and headed out to the backyard, looking for the bushes where he thought the grating had been. He got scratched up as he searched the thick bushes, experiencing two false starts before he found them.

"Right here. They're here." He began scooping up bones, working as fast as he could, filling the bucket.

"Are you okay?" Will asked as he helped.

"Nope. But what are you going to do?" No one had ever tried to kill him before. No ghost had ever tried to kill him before. Now he knew what it felt like to have dozens of... of things want you dead.

"We need to talk about what happened." Will looked concerned.

"Yeah. Not now. Now I need a bath." A bath and a few shots of whiskey and possibly a three- or four-day nap.

"Back at the hotel," Will suggested, adding more bones to a pit Darnell and Jason had dug at the side of the house. When all the bones were in the mass grave, Jason poured a box of salt from their supplies in the van onto the bones, added accelerant, and dropped a match into the pit. The flames started up, and Payne watched them silently.

Okay. Be free. Be free from that damned cellar. Leave my house and never come back.

They all waited as the fire burned down, heaving a collective sigh when the job was done. With all of them helping, it didn't take long to cover the grave.

"Thank God," murmured Darnell. "I don't ever want to go through something like that again."

"We need to debrief," Jason noted.

"Later. Later, it's been a long…." He looked at the sky. "Afternoon. For everyone. Jason might need a doctor."

"I might. Are you two going back to the hotel?" Jason looked from him to Will and back to him.

"I'm going to take a bath. I'm filthy." He was beginning to shake, his hands crusty with mud and blood. And they hurt. And dozens of people had died, and they thought he was responsible, and they'd tried to kill him.

Will put a hand on his back, running it up and down his spine. "Let me take you back to the hotel. That shower had never-ending water—you can stand in it for days."

"I'm… they tried to kill me. All of them. So many of them." Oh God, he was going to start crying.

"You know that wasn't aimed at you. They wanted Angus," Will said. "You know that."

"Still," Blaine said quietly. "The ghosts tried to kill him. He can't unsee that. For my part, I'm really sorry we made you go down there, Payne. It must have been awful."

"Yeah. I'm going inside. I don't feel well…." He turned and went back into the house—his huge, quiet, still house—and closed the door behind him. He didn't want to let the ghosts back in.

He made it to his master bathroom before he collapsed in a heap, totally overwhelmed.

Chapter Twelve

WILL started to follow Payne as he fled, but Jason grabbed his arm, stopping him.

"I'm not sure that's a good idea."

"He's in there all by himself!" Will was not leaving him alone.

"We need to take a moment to debrief."

"The ghosts in the house he loves just tried to kill him. I can't leave him to deal with this alone. I… I care about him." He needed to make sure the guys understood that. To him Payne wasn't just another customer.

"We have to get Jason looked at." Darnell was obviously worried.

"Uh-uh." Blaine shook his head. "I sort of agree with Will. What if this didn't work? I wish Payne was at a hotel."

"I'm going to stay—you guys get Jason checked out."

"I'm fine," Jason insisted.

"Yeah, but everyone else is worried, so let them take you already. I'll take care of Payne." He stopped suddenly and turned to Blaine. "Those things aren't going to try to take me over again, are they?" They'd been damn hard to fight, although the all-out takeover attempt he'd at least recognized and could fight it. The times it had turned him into an asshole had been subtler; he hadn't even realized he had something to fight when that happened. But what would happen if he went to sleep and they tried it?

"I'd be happier if you guys were at a hotel, your place, our place—anywhere not this house," Blaine admitted.

"Well, I'll try to get him to the hotel, but regardless." He wasn't leaving Payne alone. And he was guessing Payne had gone up to his room—they'd been locked up there for safety last time they were both in there, so he was hoping it was somewhere the evil ghosts couldn't get to. If they hadn't gotten them all. Surely they'd gotten them all. After all, the ghosts they'd been fighting in the basement had suddenly disappeared. Presumably when Payne got the bones out of the house. That's when they'd been able to find him in the tunnels.

"Okay. We'll call you in an hour, okay? You answer."

Will checked his phone. It was at 78 percent. "Will do." He winked at the guys so they knew the pun was intentional. Keeping it light, right? Happy, happy, joy, joy. They'd won here. Right?

Blaine came to him and hugged him. "Please be careful."

"I will. Should I drink more holy water?" He had no idea if that had helped earlier today, but he was willing.

"I don't know. I just… please, be careful."

"Okay. I'm going to go in there holding my feelings for him close, okay?" He hugged Blaine back. "Call me and let me know when the docs clear Jason."

He took a deep breath and a step back, then another step back. "Talk soon." Then he turned and headed into the house. He was going in for his lover.

The house seemed… like a house. Just a house. Quiet, but not silent, the late afternoon sun pouring in. The sunshine felt weird after what had just happened. Like there should have been a lingering dusk or something. Not that he was complaining. He didn't feel himself getting angry or grumpy or anything either. Good.

"Payne?" He was guessing Payne would have gone up to his bedroom to clean off. There had been a lot of ick on Payne from that tunnel. When he didn't get an answer, he went with his gut and went upstairs.

Payne was on the bathroom floor, tears on his cheeks, bloody hands curled into his chest.

"Oh, Professor." He lay down next to Payne and curled up around him. "I've got you. It's going to be okay."

Payne didn't respond, the sobs rocking him. Will didn't know what to do or say, so he just stayed there, petting Payne and telling him it was going to be okay. He felt pretty damn useless, to tell the truth.

Maybe he needed to get Payne clean—drag him into the tub and run the shower. Those hands needed care, cleaning, dressing.

He kissed the back of Payne's neck. "I'm going to get you cleaned up." He stood and turned on the water, letting the hot come up to temperature. Once he was happy with the heat of it, he flipped the toggle to shower. Then he undressed before moving to work on Payne's clothing. He kept up a quiet commentary the entire time so Payne would know it was him.

He hated that Payne had faced the ghosts all alone. He'd barely been able to resist their fury, their madness. It had nearly been too much. All-fucking-consuming. He shivered just thinking about it. But once the ghosts had given up on getting him and the guys join in on their quest to kill Payne, they'd focused all their attention on him. Will couldn't imagine how awful that had been.

Once he had Payne naked, he took his lover in his arms, cradling Payne against his chest.

"They hated me," Payne whispered. "They all hated me so much."

"No, Professor. It wasn't you they hated. It was Angus. You've got your grandmother and the guys. And most of all me. We all care about you and have your back." Will stepped into the shower, the hot water so good against his skin.

"They tried to…." Payne shook violently but didn't pull away this time.

"They were going after Angus, not you. They thought you were him. It was horrible, but it wasn't because of *you*." He would repeat it as many times as Payne needed to hear it.

"I could feel their hate. They were so angry and hurting. And they hated me. They would have killed me if they could have."

"But they didn't. You beat them—you freed them." He sighed and hugged Payne tight for a moment. "Let's clean off your hands, Professor. Please."

Will got Payne steady on his feet, supporting his lover's weight with his body, and brought Payne's hands into the flow of the water. He hissed as the water began to sluice off the blood and rust and dirt, knowing it had to hurt like hell. "Oh, Professor. You're torn up."

"Burns."

Yeah, he imagined it did.

"I'm going to have to wash them pretty thoroughly. Then I'll doctor them, okay? We'll look at them in the morning, and if they look infected, you'll have to go to the hospital." God knew what all Payne had wound up touching down there. "You were so brave. You managed it. You figured out what to do."

"My gram showed me. It was… overwhelming."

"She did, eh? That was her looking out for you all this time, eh?" He kissed the side of Payne's face. "Now comes the hard part. I need to soap your hands up." It was a necessary evil. To make sure they were clean. "You think she's still here?"

"I don't know. Be gentle."

"I will. I promise. Just breathe."

He was as gentle as he could be, sudsing up the soap in his own hands first, then carefully transferring the bubbles to Payne's hands and spreading it around.

Payne groaned and trembled, but he didn't pull away.

"So brave. I know it hurts, and I'm sorry." He rinsed Payne's hands off, then pulled open the shower curtain and looked at them in the brighter light. He thought maybe they needed another go. So he got his own hands all soapy and once again washed Payne's poor skin clean.

"You're going to be so sore tomorrow. Do you have Tylenol or something?"

"Uh-huh. I do. I think."

"I'll make sure you get some before you go to sleep." Will kissed his temple. "Are you sure you don't want to go to the hotel tonight? I'll pay."

He held his breath, waiting for Payne's answer. When it didn't come—neither for nor against—he sweetened the pot. "I'll order room service. Anything you want."

"Anything?"

Oh, bingo.

"That's right. Anything you want. Just name it." And if they didn't have it via room service, he'd either order it in or go pick it up himself.

"I want a cheeseburger and a milkshake."

"They are yours. We'll stop at the diner on the way to the hotel."

Payne stared at him, the expression just destroyed. "I feel so bad."

He stared back before tilting Payne's head back into the flow of water. "Tell me what's wrong, and I'll fix it."

"I've never destroyed bones before—deliberately done it to send souls to... I hope not to hell."

"You did what you had to do to save your life." If Payne hadn't gotten rid of those bones, the ghosts might have gotten all of them, not just Payne. "You saved our lives."

"It doesn't matter."

"But it does. Because it proves that you're a good man."

"I'm scared they're not gone," Payne admitted.

"You and me both. We should dry off, get dressed, and do the hotel and cheeseburger thing."

Payne nodded once. "Let's go. I'm not ready to spend the night here. Not yet."

Oh thank God. Will certainly wasn't ready either. At all, though he would have done it for Payne. He turned the water off, stepped out, and grabbed a towel so he could dry Payne off.

"Did you ever find that first aid kit?"

"I did. It's in the linen closet."

"Okay. Go sit on the bed, and I'll get it." He gave Payne a quick kiss on the top of his head, then wrapped a towel around his waist and went to find the first aid kit.

Payne was curled up on the bed when he got back, head on his pillow. Will sat down and stroked Payne's damp hair away from his face. He hated how sad and scared and defeated Payne looked.

"I'm sorry," he said again. "I wish it had been me they'd been after."

"I'm glad it wasn't." Payne reached out for him with one of those torn-up hands.

He slid his fingers along the back of Payne's hand. "Let's take care of these." He found the Polysporin in the first aid kit and splooched a bunch on Payne's torn-up hands. "I'm worried about you getting an infection."

"Yeah, me too."

"Did you want me to take you to the hospital instead of the hotel?" It probably would be the responsible thing to do.

"No. No hospital. I just want food and rest."

"Okay. Food and rest it is." He slathered the Polysporin on both of Payne's hands, then wrapped them gently in gauze. "There you go."

"Thanks. Can you drive?"

"Yeah, I can." He kissed the backs of Payne's hands. "Let's get you fed."

He helped Payne up and led him to the door. He turned the handle and pulled, and the damn thing stuck. "Oh, for fuck's sake, Grandma. Let us out." He yanked on the door again, and this time it opened for him.

"Maybe it was just sticking," Payne suggested.

"Maybe so." He didn't care. He'd been manipulated more than enough by the ghosts in this house.

He put his hand on Payne's lower back and led him out of the bedroom and down the stairs. Everything looked so normal, so peaceful. It was hard to believe what had gone on in the basement had actually happened. The whole thing had felt like a terrible nightmare that he couldn't wake up from. He didn't think he'd ever forget the feeling of the ghosts trying to wriggle into his mind, into his soul.

The keys to Payne's car were on the table in the front hall, along with his wallet. Will slipped the wallet into Payne's back pocket and grabbed the keys.

"Let's go feed you. Burgers. Milkshakes."

"Works for me." Payne rolled his head on his shoulders, the bones creaking and popping.

"I'll give you a massage when we get to the hotel. After we've eaten," Will suggested.

Payne nodded. "I might just take another shower and make the hot water do the work."

"If you'd prefer doing that, sure. But I'd like to. You might have noticed—I like touching you." He got Payne bundled in the car, then headed toward the Silver Flyer.

Payne seemed quiet, his hands held carefully in his lap.

"So, I guess we'll need to come back and make sure all the ghosts are gone, eh?" He wished Payne would sell up and find somewhere else to live, actually. Then it wouldn't matter if the bone cleansing had worked or not. Of course, there was that clause that said he couldn't do that.

"Yeah. Or at least the mean ones. Gram can stay."

"Weirdest conversation with a special someone ever," Will noted.

Payne chuckled, the sound tired, drawn. "Things have been utterly fucked up all right."

"I think things were fucked up for you for a lot longer than just today."

"Yeah. Yeah, I guess so. I wish I'd never brought you in."

"What? You can't mean that!" Payne had been miserable, sleeping badly, and the ghosts had been playing havoc with his life. Not to mention, him and Payne....

"You were in danger. Seriously. I hate that."

"Oh." He reached over and touched Payne's knee. He liked that Payne was protective of him. It was a new feeling, but it warmed him through. "But if you hadn't called us in, you and I would never have met. And you'd still have a ghost problem. Those things seriously thought you were Angus, and they wanted you dead." It made him shiver again, remember the uncontrolled rage that had tried to take him over, that had tried to make him kill Payne. He'd fought them, though. His feelings for Payne had been stronger, in the end.

"Yeah." Payne sighed. "That just... yeah."

"You know it wasn't you they really wanted dead, right?" He was going to keep reminding Payne of that until Payne really believed it. He was pretty sure they weren't there yet. "You didn't do anything to them. And you aren't responsible for what your ancestor did."

"Of course I wasn't. I'm not him. Not a bit. I'm a librarian."

Will was suddenly tickled. Librarian, like that said it all. Maybe it did. "Maybe it's the librarian in you, or maybe it's you, eh? You'd be a good guy no matter what you did for a living."

"Don't you mean stuffy and boring?"

He was going to pinch Payne.

"Dude. Stop that. I know today was hard, but you are a good guy, and you're hot, and you're sexy."

"I'm not feeling particularly sexy today."

"You don't have to feel it to be it. I promise."

Payne shot him a half smile, so that was something, right?

They pulled up at the diner. "You want to eat here or bring it to the hotel with us?"

"Can we please take it to go?"

"I was hoping you'd say that." They went in and walked to the counter to put in their order. "You want a milkshake while we wait for our food to come?"

"Yeah. Vanilla please."

They ordered an extra pair of shakes, which the waitress made for them right away. He watched Payne sucking on the straw, admiring him. Payne's color began to improve as he drank.

Will's phone went off—text from the guys. He passed the news on to Payne as he texted back, letting them know that he'd gotten Payne out of the house for the night. "Jason's got the all clear from the doctor."

"Excellent. I'm glad. Seriously."

It still felt like Payne was a million miles away. Will wasn't sure what to do, how to reach out. He knew what had happened in the basement had been fucking traumatic. He just wasn't sure how to help. They didn't make a card for "sorry the ghosts in your house tried to kill you."

Payne sighed softly. "Man, I have to admit, I'm sore everywhere. It's like I worked hard or something."

"Your hands would agree that you worked hard. I just hope they don't get infected."

"Me too. I don't want to have to go to the hospital."

"Yeah, it'd be pretty hard to explain what happened without getting yourself locked in the looney bin."

"Exactly. It would be awkward at best."

Will reached out and slid his little finger alongside Payne's. It might have been a tiny touch, but it gave him a point of connection. Payne's finger curled, squeezed his for a second. He felt that all through his body, and he gave Payne a smile.

He sucked on his own milkshake, enjoying the cold as it traveled down his throat and into his belly. He could understand why Payne was perking up; the ice cream was healing a number of spiritual wounds.

They'd almost finished their milkshakes when their takeout showed up, including a new set of shakes. Perfect. They finished off the shakes they already had, and he gave Payne the bag of food. Then he grabbed the travel tray with the shakes in one hand and Payne's free hand in the other. He was looking forward to being alone in a safe place with Payne where they could decompress together.

It didn't take them any time at all. The hotel was just up the road, and they had all his and Payne's information already in the system from the previous night. They even had the same room available. Will and Payne made their way up, and as soon as they were in the room, Will set the shakes on the side table and took the bag of food from Payne, putting it down on the bed. He took the two takeout boxes out of the bag and opened them. The smell of the cheeseburgers and fries wafted up, making his stomach growl.

Payne sat cross-legged on the bed. "Thank you for this. I needed something stupidly normal."

Will got that. He really did. They usually went back to Blaine's after a ghost hunt and had pizza, something normal and easy, and then they'd decompress. "Whatever you need, Professor." He sat with his feet dangling.

"What I need is for my house to just be my house."

"Well, I can't promise we did that today, but I think we did. We'll all have to get together tomorrow and go through the house with the instruments. Make sure we got them all." He wasn't letting Payne go home alone. Not as long as there was a chance it wasn't over.

"Yeah. I hope it worked. Seriously. I feel like someone got closure anyway."

"Yeah? Did you feel your grandmother at all before we left? I mean, if that wasn't her sticking your bedroom door closed. Do you think she'll be gone now too if we got rid of the ones that were out for you?" Will kind of hoped she would be, for her sake as well as Payne's. She deserved to rest in peace, and Payne deserved to live in a ghost-free home after what had happened.

"I don't know. Really. I don't even know what I hope," Payne admitted.

"Well, let's chow down and cuddle and have a nonghosty, not the house, just us regular old time. I bet everything looks better in the morning after that and a good night's sleep." He knew Payne hadn't been sleeping well at all ever since the whole ghost thing had started.

Payne picked up his cheeseburger carefully and Will watched to make sure he didn't have any trouble with the burger. He seemed to be managing fine. So Will snuck one of Payne's fries, grinning because he had exactly the same stuff in his own takeout container.

"Hands off, man." Payne swatted at him, then went back to eating carefully with his bandaged hands.

Will couldn't tell if the swat was playful or not. So he just concentrated on his burger for a bit, enjoying the particular greasy flavor that existed nowhere else but in a cheeseburger. Before stealing another fry. This time he got a chuckle before the swat.

He grinned and stole one more.

"Butthead. My fries are disappearing at an alarming rate."

"Alarming? I've had three." Will was trying, but he couldn't keep the grin off his face. "You should totally steal some of mine—they taste better when they're off someone else's plate." It was a known fact.

"Feed me, Seymour." Payne opened his mouth like a hungry bird.

Will checked out his fries and found the choicest one. Grabbing it, he held it up to Payne's lips. Payne ate it, humming low, and okay, that felt good. And now Will's eyes were glued to Payne's lips. So pretty, especially with a slight gloss from where Payne had licked them.

He picked up another fry, this time without checking as his eyes were otherwise occupied, and offered it over as well.

"Thank you." God, how sweet. Payne ate it, tongue sliding on his fingertips.

Will groaned, his body tightening immediately. That he wanted this man and that it had nothing to do with that house or ghosts was clear. Every moment he spent away from the house, he liked Payne more.

"You want another one?" He had to clear his throat, his words all gruff.

"Uh-huh. Please. One more."

"You can have as many as you want." He looked this time, making sure he picked another great one. Then he took a small bite before offering the rest of it over to Payne.

"Oh fuck this." Payne pushed into his arms and kissed him, good and hard.

He opened his mouth wide, letting Payne in as he slid his hands along Payne's shoulders. A shudder went through him. It felt so good touching Payne, trying to make him feel good. He wanted Payne to feel good.

Payne pushed back against Will's hands, letting him feel, letting him in.

Will shoved the takeout containers to the end of the bed, glad that they'd left the milkshakes on the side table. Then he pushed Payne back onto the bed and followed him down.

"Hey." Payne held on to him, and that had to be hurting those poor hands.

"Why don't you lie back and let me do the work. Save your hands for another day?" He took one and kissed the back of it, the gauze feeling strange, almost ticklish, against his lips. "Let me make you feel good."

"If you want to...." Payne sounded so unsure.

He lay half on Payne, half on the mattress and stroked Payne's cheek. "Why wouldn't I want to?" Payne knew Will liked him. A lot. Right? The craziness at the house hadn't changed that for him. In fact, it maybe made him like Payne even more because it had shown him Payne's strength, his ability to survive, be smart, be strong.

Be in the middle of things and not panic.

"I don't know. I don't know anything right now."

"Then just lie back and let me love on you." He put Payne's hands down by his sides and pressed on his wrists, silently communicating that Payne should keep them down there. Then he started with a kiss on Payne's lips, his tongue lingering, teasing them. He could taste the salt from the french fries, and it added to the deliciousness that was Payne. Soft moans filled the air, Payne shifting underneath him, begging for him.

Will liked that, and he wanted to hear more. He was going to make Payne forget everything but his touch. And he was going to make it last too. He nuzzled Payne's neck, licking the soft skin there.

Payne shivered. "Sensitive."

Yeah, he knew.

He licked there again, taking Payne's flavor in, loving how it was different yet the same. As he licked and nibbled, he slid his hands down Payne's torso and played with the bottom of his shirt. He tugged it out of Payne's slacks before slowly pushing it up. His fingertips danced along Payne's skin. So soft, so warm. He loved touching this man.

"If it was my gram who locked us in my room, she had the right idea," Payne whispered.

"Yeah? You think she locked us in your room because she knew we belonged together and needed each other?"

"Either that or she saw how studly you are."

Will chuckled. "You think I'm a stud, eh?"

"Does anyone not think you're a stud? Seriously?"

"I've heard it said that I'm too short." Not that he let it bother him. He was pretty okay with himself. And if Payne happened to think he was a stud, he would totally take it.

"You're beautiful. Seriously."

"You know you've already got me, eh?" Still, he liked hearing it from Payne. "Not to mention, you're very handsome."

"Skinny and pale, more like it."

Oh no. Lean and wonderful and fine.

"Do I argue with you when you tell me I'm a beautiful stud? No, I do not. So when I tell you that you're handsome and lovely, lean and wonderful, you believe it." He growled a little for effect.

"You.... Okay. Fine, I guess." Payne pinched one of his nipples.

Gasping, he pinched one of Payne's, tugging a little on the nipple ring he'd almost forgotten about.

Not too hard, though. No pain for his Payne. He bit his lip to keep from giggling at the thought.

"Mmm." Payne tugged gently, stroking Will's nipple more than pinching this time.

Will groaned. This would be so much better if…. Pulling away, he tugged off his shirt and tossed it across the room. Then he pulled Payne's off too. "Better." Grinning, he slid his fingers across both of Payne's nipples. "So much better."

"I want you to help me fly, Will. I want to let today go."

"There's nothing I want more." Making love and having that be what Payne needed to help him through the whole shitshow they'd been through earlier sounded like just what the doctor ordered, for both of them.

He dropped kisses over Payne's face, the odd one landing on Payne's lips, then moved on to adore Payne's throat in the same manner. Payne swallowed and moaned, Adam's apple bobbing under Will's lips.

Someone needed him. It was a heady sensation, and his cock was growing with every passing second. Pushing at his jeans like it was going to tear through the denim. He pressed his groin to Payne's, groaning as he rubbed their hard pricks together. He so should have pulled their jeans off at the same time as he got rid of their shirts.

He couldn't even ask Payne to help with the buttons; his hands were all bandaged up.

He backed away. "Last interruption," he promised. Then he opened Payne's top button and carefully pulled the zipper down. Grabbing the waistband, he tugged both jeans and underwear down, pulling them off Payne's hips and ass, then down his legs. Payne arched for him, clearly eager to help.

"I like how you think, Will. My cock didn't fit anymore."

"Oh, I think it's going to fit just fine." He was going in for a taste. First he licked the head, tongue lingering on Payne's slit.

"I meant.... Oh... Will...." Payne arched up, bucking into Will's lips. "Damn!"

Okay, that worked. He opened up and let Payne spread his lips, the hard cock pushing into his mouth. He didn't think Payne was thinking about ghosts right now.

No ghosts, no spirits, no fear.

Just Will's mouth—heat and pleasure and tight lips.

He flicked his tongue across the head of Payne's cock as he pulled up, then he bobbed his head back down, taking in as much as he could before starting the upward drag again.

Payne bent one knee and cradled him. "God, do it again. Please."

Oh, he was going to do it again. And again. And again. All the way to Payne's orgasm. He hummed his reply, slapped the head of Payne's cock with his tongue, then took him in deep once more. Payne rolled up, shoulders leaving the mattress.

It made Will feel powerful that he could make this sexy man so wild, so wanton and needy. With another happy hum, he repeated the sequence time and again.

"More. More. Touch me," Payne begged.

He loved Payne's need, loved that it was strong enough to set his lover begging.

As he continued to suck Payne off, he slid his fingers up the smooth belly, slowly teasing his way toward that one ringed nipple.

"Yes." Payne wasn't shy at all. "Please."

He grabbed hold of the ring and tugged it gently, trying to smile around Payne's cock at the way Payne arched for him. Hell yes. Soon he was going to bury himself in Payne, bring them together, push them over the edge.

First he wanted Payne's come in his mouth, and to that end he sucked harder and bobbed his head faster. He played with the ring, but also with Payne's bare nipple, giving it equal attention.

Payne began to cry out, warning him that his climax was coming. That spurred him to try even harder to get Payne to come. He wanted the flood of spunk to fill his mouth. He wanted to taste that salty, bitter Payne flavor. He wanted it burned into his brain.

"Will!" Seed poured into him, Payne giving him everything, offering himself up.

He took it all in, swallowing around the head of Payne's cock. This was what he'd wanted, and he wasn't disappointed, not at all.

Payne collapsed back, panting furiously. "Damn."

Will pulled off slowly, then took a moment to lick Payne clean, making sure to get every single drop and to sample every single bit of flesh with his tongue.

Payne blinked down at him, eyes dazed. Will smiled up at his lover, then slowly licked Payne again, from his balls to the tip of his cock. He kissed his way along Payne's belly, up the middle of his rib cage to his breastbone. Then he had to decide—ringed or unringed nipple first. He went for the unringed nipple, wrapping his lips around it and pulling gently.

"You... you're real?" Payne's moan was so happy, blissful.

"I'm fucking real, Professor." He kissed his way over to the ringed nipple and wasn't gentle with this one, grabbing the nipple between his teeth and tugging on it.

"Will!" Payne gasped and arched.

"You still wanting? Because I am. I want to be buried inside you, filling you up, feeling you around me."

"Take me. I can go again." Payne spread wide, pulling his knees up and back.

Will groaned at the clear and open invitation. He bent, licking along Payne's crack, right to his hole. He laved it with his tongue, wetting it on the outside in anticipation of doing the same on the inside. Each swipe made Payne twist and groan, the sound desperate.

He licked his way into Payne's hole, the muscles there gripping his tongue tight. He hummed again, making Payne buck, then began to tongue-fuck his lover. He moved quickly, knowing his tongue was going to get tired quickly and wanting to be sure he got Payne good and slick.

He wanted to sink into Payne, to fuck his lover until they both screamed.

Payne whimpered. "Making me crazy, Will."

He took that as his sign and pulled away. He grabbed his jeans from the floor and pulled out his wallet, finding the condom he knew would be there. Making short work of getting it on, he was soon gloved up and pressing against Payne's spit-slick hole.

Payne pushed up toward him, taking him in with a single wild push. Will's eyes rolled back in his head, the pleasure almost too big. He didn't want to come yet. He wanted to spend as much time as he could right here, thrusting into Payne over and over.

It took a few breaths, but he found some control, and that let him start moving.

"You're… you're something else. So deep." Payne kept muttering as he tossed his head.

Will took it all in, loving every second—the tight heat around his cock, the semicoherent words of his lover. It all worked to send him toward his orgasm, making his body sing.

Payne met every plunge, every single push and tug.

Will got his hand around Payne's cock while he still had the sense to do so and tugged in time with each of his thrusts. He could hear his own breath echoing in his head, playing the beat for the rhythm he was building.

It was so easy to get lost here, buried in Payne. So easy and so good.

Bending, he brought their mouths together, and that changed his angle, stimulating his cock in a new way. He cried out into Payne's mouth, hammering home now, racing to his finish. Payne took him, every inch, slamming them together.

All of a sudden he was coming, his body jerking into Payne's a few more times as the spunk shot out of him. He squeezed his hand around Payne's cock as aftershocks rocked him.

A dribble of seed escaped Payne's prick, and a low moan left Payne's throat.

Groaning, Will let Payne hold his weight as he panted, trying to catch his breath. Damn, that had been spectacular.

Payne blinked at him, nice and slow.

Will wished he didn't have to pull out, but it would be messy and make having worn the condom meaningless if he didn't, so he slipped out, tossed the condom, and glommed back on to Payne.

"You good, Professor?"

"Uh-huh. Good as I'm ever going to be."

Will kissed him softly, then laid his head next to Payne's. He stroked the lovely belly. "'Kay. Good. Cuddle now."

Payne nodded, snuggling close. "Cuddle."

Half asleep already, Will sighed with satisfaction. "My professor."

Chapter Thirteen

PAYNE woke up with a start, the sensation of being chased pushing him out of his dreams.

"Fuck!"

Will popped up next to him, looking around wildly. "What? What is it? Payne?"

"Will." Oh. Oh, God. Okay. "Sorry. Nightmare."

He scrubbed his face, the gauze on his hands rough and catching on his stubble.

"I bet I can guess what it was about too." Will wrapped around him, arms warm and solid. It felt like nothing could get to him when Will held him like this.

"Yeah. Well, yesterday was… whoa." He went for light.

"Just a little." Will rolled his eyes, then gave him a tight squeeze. "They're gone, though. You beat them.

We'll confirm it tom—" Will looked at the clock on the bedside table. "Almost seven, wow. Today, then, I guess."

"Today. I can't spend my life in a hotel, and it's a great house, right?"

"It's a gorgeous house. Without the horde of nasties, it'll be perfect. You want me to text the guys and see what the plan is?" Will's hand rested on Payne's thigh, reminding him he wasn't facing this alone.

"Are they going to be awake? If not, let's check out and go find somewhere amazing for breakfast."

"I like that idea. Let's do it, and we'll text them from there." Will grabbed one of his hands. "Let's check these out first, eh?"

"Only if they're looking okay, huh?" He went for light and clever. He didn't want to have to go to the hospital.

"So if they aren't, we'll just wrap them back up and pretend we didn't look in the first place?"

"Works for me!" He winked, and they both found a laugh.

Will settled down and unwrapped his right hand carefully. "Oh. That's not too bad at all."

When all was said and done, the cuts were sore but obviously not septic, and Payne made do with some bandages and a little more antibiotic.

Will kissed the back of his hands. "Thank God the bad memories and scratched-up but not infected hands are the worst of it." That it could have been so much worse was left unsaid.

The worry was that it wasn't over, but Payne guessed they had to have hope.

They left the hotel hand in hand, Will holding his so gently. "Mel's up on the left there looks like it might be a winner. One of those surprising little mom-and-pop shops."

"I'm a diner person. Let's do it." They packed the car and walked over to the little hole in the wall.

For all it was tiny and totally nondescript outside, they walked into a warm and cozy restaurant that seemed really homey. A cheerful woman greeted them.

"Sit anywhere you'd like. There's menus on the tables. You boys want coffee?"

"Please," Will answered for both of them.

"And orange juice, please." Payne thought that would clear his mind.

"Make it two." Will grinned and pointed to a little booth against the far wall. "Look good?"

He nodded, and they headed over, sitting across from each other. It felt so normal. Like they were lovers having breakfast out, nothing more.

Payne wondered if that could ever be true, be real. God, he hoped so. He hoped that the ghosts were gone and gone for good, and that he could enjoy his home and his new lover without anyone wanting him dead and trying to get him there.

Will's feet slid against his under the table. It was such a small thing, but it was a connection, and it felt good because of that.

Will picked up a menu. "What do you feel like?"

"Bacon and waffles, I think." He wanted something comforting and sweet and salty all at once. "I'm stressed out, huh?"

"I know." Will grabbed his hand and squeezed very gently. "Let me text the guys and see if we can expedite scanning for ghosts." Will pulled out his phone. "You want to do the run-through with us or stay in the car, or even here in town?"

"I should be there. I want to be able to believe it's okay. I want to sleep in my own bed and not be the guy ghosts are trying to kill because they think I'm evil and cruel and want to hurt them."

"You're the gentlest man I know," Will said. "Of course you wouldn't hurt them. It's because you look like Angus and they're ghosts. I can't explain this stuff as well as Blaine can, but ghosts don't understand the passage of time. It's like they're stuck at the moment they died, yeah? They don't get it. Didn't get it, because with any luck they're dead and gone for real now."

"Have you seen something like this before?" Payne asked. It would help to know that Will and the others knew of other cases.

"You mean vengeful spirits like this? Sort of. That hospital case we mentioned, the ghost wanted revenge on his brother, who kept him from being with his lover. But never one with so many like your ghosts. It makes sense, though, if they all died together or around the same time and for the same reason, that they'd mesh together into one big nasty mob of ghosts."

"Do you think they killed my gram? Or was that her great-grandfather?"

"I don't know. Neither option is very appealing, is it? But my guess is that Angus wasn't still around. Why would he be? And what good would it do him to kill her? I think she stayed around because she knew about the ghosts in the basement and wanted to protect you. Because she loved you."

Payne mulled that over for a minute. "I guess so," he said finally. "She picked kind of a scary way to do it, though. Was it her moving things around and throwing things, or was that the bad ghosts?"

"We may never know for sure, but I think that was her." Will shrugged. "Blaine says ghosts have a hard time communicating. Maybe she was trying to scare you away from the house at first, and when that didn't work, all she could do was try to keep you from going down to the basement. It seems like the angry spirits were contained down there. They could affect things through us mentally, like they did with me, but they couldn't do anything physical upstairs. We all thought it was the bad ghosts trying to keep you out of the basement at first. But look how they went after you when you did get down there. No, I bet she was doing everything she could to keep you out of harm's way."

"I saw her, you know," Payne told Will. "She was downstairs. She helped me."

Will squeezed Payne's hand gently once more, and even though Payne's hand was pretty sore, that squeeze sent warmth all through him.

"Okay," Will said. He raised his phone and started messaging. "I'll tell the guys you want to be there." He grinned. "You know, you're our honorary team member this time around. We've never had someone not part of the group doing everything with us before. Of course this was our first time in a building that wasn't abandoned."

"I just want to have peace. Did you get anything for your show?"

"I'll be shocked if we didn't. I'll ask the guys when we've figured out when and where we're meeting and stuff." Will kept texting, fingers flying over the keys.

"Right." Soon he'd be home, alone in the house, trying to put things back together.

The waitress came by to drop off their drinks and take their order before Will was done with his message, but he stopped long enough to ask for the Full Farmer's Breakfast. Payne placed his own order, and she promised them it wouldn't be long.

Will finally put down his phone. "They're going to meet us at the house after breakfast. So we can give you your all clear as soon as possible."

"Okay. What... what happens then?" Did Will just disappear from his life?

"Then the Supers will get out of your hair, and Jason will work on editing what we've got into a cohesive show. For my part, I hope you'll let me continue to prove that we have something together that has nothing to do with the house. Just you and me."

"Yeah?" Because that was important. "The you-and-me part."

"Unless you don't want to." Will frowned like that idea had only just occurred to him. "In which case, I'll be spending time trying to convince you to give me a chance. I really do care for you, Payne. I know we've only known each other short time, but our relationship was forged in the midst of turmoil, and that always cements things faster." Will stopped talking and nudged his leg under the table. "Put me out of my misery and tell me you are serious about me too."

"I am. I want to give you all the chances." He wanted Will in his bed.

"Thank God." Will laughed softly and took his hand, holding it gently. "I want to know if our chemistry works in your bed as well as it does at the hotel." Will waggled his eyebrows. "Hell, I'll even be happy to invite you to mine, although it's a hovel compared to your house."

"I'd like you to fall in love with the house. It's honestly a magical place."

"Yeah? That doesn't surprise me, because the man who owns it is pretty damn magical in my books."

"Flatterer. It's going to be all right, isn't it?"

"I want it to be all right. I think that counts for a lot. You're not a client to me, and you're not just a friend with benefits. I care about you. And I want you to be happy. I want you to live in a safe place. Hell, I want to live in a safe place, and I have to admit to hoping… that you'll have me."

"Yeah? After two days?" Because he would, and not because he was scared to be alone either.

"I know that's what people are going to say, but our relationship was…. What's that expression? Forged in fire. And I feel like I know you better than I know a lot of other people who I've known a lot longer. So yes, after two days. And if you need more time, that's cool. I have faith in how I feel, and I have staying power."

"I have a lot of room, you know. You could… have an office even."

"An office? You mean for the Supers? Like, an honest-to-God office?"

"Yeah, I mean… is that too much? I've never fallen in love before…."

The wonder in Will's face morphed into joy. "You've fallen in love with me? Because I'm falling in love with you."

"People are going to say we're insane." Not that he cared, but it was true.

"Professor, me and my friends hunt ghosts. I'm used to people thinking I'm insane." Will grinned and bounced in his seat like a kid. "You're giving me an office for the Supers. And you love me. And I'm moving into your house with you. I get to wake up with you every day."

"Even if it's haunted by my meddling gram?"

"Are you kidding? Your gram loves me."

Payne tilting his head. "She does?"

"She was the first one to put us together. You remember being locked safely in your room for a day? That was totally her."

"Dear Grandson, here's your man. Love, Gram?"

"You've gotta admit—she's got great taste!"

Payne began to laugh, his tension leaving him in a rush. Will watched him with a sweet, indulgent look on his face.

Before either of them could say anything, their breakfast arrived, plates full of food that smelled amazing.

He thought maybe he could finally relax and eat.

Relax, eat, and then go home. He looked up, finding Will looking at him with a goofy grin.

"Dig in, Professor. Then we'll go home."

Chapter Fourteen

WILL was in a damn fine mood. He was behind the camera as they went through the MacGregor house. Blaine was narrating, talking about the differences between yesterday and today.

So far, they hadn't even felt Payne's gram's presence. Of courses, they hadn't tried to go into the basement yet. He thought that was going to be the real test. And they were headed right for it, now, having cleared the kitchen.

Jason waved for Payne to approach the basement door with him, and Will kept a close eye on his lover through the camera. More to make sure Payne was okay than to film it for the Supers. Which was maybe a dereliction of his duty or something, but he didn't care. Payne was his priority.

"We're at the basement door now," Jason noted. "Payne, do you feel anything strange?"

"No. No, I feel... nervous because of yesterday, but that's it."

"Nobody is telling you not to go downstairs?" Jason asked. "No threats to you or your friends if you go down?"

"No. I just feel... like me." Payne grinned a little. "I'm going to go down and see what happens. I expect saving if I don't come back."

Will grunted. Payne was not going down there on his own. No way, no how. Jason and Blaine were right there with him, thank God.

"Oh, we're coming too. We need to film, and you need the extra flashlight power. You can go first, though, if you'd like."

That didn't make Will happy, but he was going as well, so he didn't complain. He was ready to jump to Payne's defense, though, should there be even a hint of danger.

Payne looked toward the camera, but Will knew he was looking at *him*. "Let's do this."

He grinned at his man. Look at Payne, taking the bull by the horns and going down to the very place where yesterday God knew how many ghosts had tried to take him out. Will was so proud.

Payne headed down the stairs and they all followed.

He couldn't breathe for a second as he reached the bottom of the stairs, but it didn't last. He sucked in air and looked at the other guys, who all seemed to be in the same boat.

Payne surged forward, though, as if he hadn't been the guy who'd been targeted and almost killed by the ghosts who'd been after the original MacGregor.

A mist built between Payne and the rest of them, a faint shimmer.

"Fuck." Will headed down the stairs at breakneck speed, pushing past the guys who were ahead of him.

Payne reached for him, chuckling softly. "He's right here, Gram. He's here. See?"

"Jesus, I thought you were about to be attacked again." Will rested his hand on Payne's shoulder and pressed his forehead against Payne's. "Does she believe they're gone?"

"I don't know, but she's gone now too, see? She wanted to know you were here."

Will looked around. Payne was right; the shimmering was gone. "So she left once she knew you weren't alone?" He was thinking that was better than her hanging around. He had a hunch he'd have performance issues if he knew she could pop up at any moment.

"I think she's happy. It felt like she was happy."

"I think that means the others are all gone." Will turned to the guys. "You hear that? Payne's gram's ghost was here to make sure he wasn't alone, then she left. She wouldn't do that if there were still any danger, right?"

Blaine nodded slowly, getting that faraway look. "I'd have to agree. The ghosts are gone. I can't feel them."

"It's not very scientific," Flynn noted. "Going by whether or not someone's grandmother's ghost is happy or not."

"Yeah, let's do our exploration of the basement with the camera and all the instruments. That way we can draw some educated conclusions." Jason headed determinedly toward the right.

Payne nodded. "Do what you need to."

Then Payne grabbed Will and kissed him good and hard.

The other guys all gaped, but Will just smiled and aimed the camera in their general direction as he kissed his lover.

"I think you're home free, Professor," he whispered.

"I think *we* are. Welcome home, Will."

"Thank you, Professor."

Will gave Payne one last kiss before focusing back on his camera and following after the guys. They had to keep filming for the show, but it didn't matter. He knew they wouldn't find anything. His boyfriend's ghost grandma had said so.

Now Available

(ᗞREAMSPUN BEYOND

The Supers

By Sean Michael
The Supers

Hunting ghosts and finding more than they bargained for.

Blaine Franks is a member of the paranormal research group the Supernatural Explorers. When the group loses their techie to a cross-country move, newly graduated Flynn Huntington gets the job. Flynn fits in with the guys right off the bat, but when it comes to him and Blaine, it's more than just getting along.

Things heat up between Blaine and Flynn as they explore their first haunted building, an abandoned hospital, together. Their relationship isn't all that progresses, though, and soon it seems that an odd bite on Blaine's neck has become much more.

Hitchhiking ghosts, a tragic love story forgotten by time, and the mystery of room 204 round out a romance where the things that go bump in the night are real.

Coming in November 2018

DREAMSPUN BEYOND

Dreamspun Beyond #31
Fangs for the Memories by Julia Talbot

One wolf lost his memory, but they'll both lose their hearts.

Bitten werewolf Tom owes the folks at the Dead and Breakfast big for saving his life. So when they ask for help with a rogue wolf on the premises, he's happy to do his part….

Though he isn't quite prepared for what he'll find.

Werewolf Nathan lost everything to a sadistic kidnapper—his freedom, his memories, and maybe even his ability to be human. But as soon as he meets Tom, he knows he might be able to reclaim his life. And even a turned wolf like Tom feels the mating call. The trouble is, Tom isn't the only one who wants Nathan, and they'll need help from all their supernatural friends at the D & B to defeat a powerful enemy and keep their love—and themselves—alive.

Dreamspun Beyond #32
Quenched in Blood by Ari McKay

Will love mean rebirth… or death?

Vampire Julian Schaden has been warning the Asheville Paranormal Council of an impending demonic incursion for more than two decades. Over the past two years, he and his friends have fought as hard as they can with little help, since Micah Carter, the demon hunter who should have led them, shirked his responsibility and then perished.

Desperate for anything that might aid the fight, Julian enters the Carter property and finds something he never dared hope for: young Thomas Carter, the heir to a long line of demon hunters.

Thomas knows nothing about the supernatural world. But the prospect of a real life, outside the sheltered, isolated farm where he grew up, calls to him, and the idea of fighting the Unholy feels right.

Julian agrees to train Thomas, but he struggles against an unexpected, unwanted attraction. Thomas is too young and innocent to get involved with Julian, but opposites attract, and this is one battle Julian seems fated to lose. But a prophecy from a dying mage comes with a bleak warning: the upcoming battle will claim Thomas's life. To keep his home and friends safe, Julian may have to sacrifice the only love he's ever known.